'There's a ⸺ **e fridge. Wh** ⸺ **a glass? I'll read Heidi a story and put her to bed,' Hannah said.**

When Hannah didn't reappear Adam wandered back into the living area. Evidence of a small child in residence was everywhere. A tiny table with matching chair took up a corner of the room and a dolls' house took up another. A well-nibbled and soggy biscuit sat on the arm of the couch. It was the abandoned biscuit that caught a raw nerve. Déjà vu.

Adam moved into the hallway. Hearing the soft murmur of Hannah's voice, he was drawn to an open door.

'...and the tiniest bear never lost its squeak ever again, because there was always somebody there to hug him.'

'Queek me, Mumma!'

Adam paused in the doorway. He saw Hannah fold her arms around the child and the emotional tug he felt was poignant enough to be physically painful.

Alison Roberts was born in New Zealand, and she says, 'I lived in London and Washington DC as a child, and began my working career as a primary school teacher. A lifelong interest in medicine was fostered by my doctor and nurse parents, flatting with doctors and physiotherapists on leaving home, and marriage to a house surgeon who is now a cardiologist. I have also worked as a cardiology technician and research assistant. My husband's medical career took us to Glasgow for two years, which was an ideal place and time to start my writing career. I now live in Christchurch, New Zealand, with my husband, daughter and various pets.'

Recent titles by the same author:

NURSE IN NEED
TWICE AS GOOD
A PERFECT RESULT
AN IRRESISTIBLE INVITATION

EMOTIONAL RESCUE

BY
ALISON ROBERTS

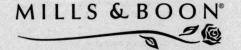

MILLS & BOON®

First published in Great Britain 2001
Harlequin Mills & Boon Limited,
Eton House, 18-24 Paradise Road, Richmond, Surrey TW9 1SR

© Alison Roberts 2001

ISBN 0 263 82679 1

Set in Times Roman 10½ on 12 pt.
03-0801-47716

Printed and bound in Spain
by Litografia Rosés, S.A., Barcelona

CHAPTER ONE

NOTHING had ever felt this good.

Hannah Duncan basked in the warmth of the summer evening's last rays of sunshine. The accumulated heat captured by the shingle of the beach she was sitting on dispelled the final chill from her swim in the lake water. Her eyes were closed, her face raised in appreciation of the sun's caress. No breath of wind interrupted the welcome radiance.

Hannah opened her eyes only reluctantly but the addition of another sense did not disturb the profound peacefulness of the scene. The fading sunlight bathed the distant mountains and the lake with a rosy glow. Now that the group of boisterous children had given up their game on the lake's shallow edge, the water had stilled enough to reflect the trees that grew just beyond the beach. A young couple lay on the grass beneath the trees, more absorbed in each other than the picturesque sunset. Hannah smiled. She knew exactly how they felt.

Unconsciously, her hand went to her stomach, still flat even beneath the thin fabric of her swimsuit. Only she and Ben knew what the flatness concealed, and it was a secret they intended to keep, at least until the end of this idyllic holiday. Hannah's gaze eagerly sought Ben who had ignored the chilly water in favour of continuing their dip. Even her fiancé had now been caught by the perfect sense of peace. Not swimming any more, he floated on his back, his arms outstretched—his body so still that no ripples marred the glassy surface of the lake.

5

Hannah was tempted to call out but couldn't bring herself to break the absolute silence. The happy cries of the children had gone as soon as they'd dispersed into the outskirts of the camping ground. Even the birds had suddenly ceased their evening calls.

The chill that gripped Hannah at that point had little to do with the fading light. The goose-bumps that erupted on her body could not be attributed to any puff of breeze. The cry to catch Ben's attention was now caught by a painful constriction in Hannah's throat. Ben wasn't floating on his back at all. He was face down.

He was...*drowning*!

Had she screamed or was it simply an echo that resounded in her own head? Something quickly alerted the young couple. The man ran to help Hannah, diving into the lake as the depth began to slow his pace. The woman ran towards the camping ground and it seemed as though the crowd had gathered well before they managed to drag Ben onto the shingle beach.

How could there be so many people and yet nobody knew what they should do?

'There's an ambulance coming,' someone said.

'I don't think he's breathing.' Someone else sounded horrified.

Hannah knelt beside Ben, her hands cupping his face. Of course he wasn't breathing. How long had he been face down in the water, unable to breathe, while she had simply been sitting—basking in that deceptively evil calm? And now, when it was so important, Hannah had no real idea of what she should *do*.

'Give him the kiss of life,' a male voice ordered. 'I'll push on his chest. I've seen it on television often enough.'

Ben's lips were so cold. Hannah could feel the warmth of her own breath as it entered his mouth. She could feel it again as it escaped, pushed out by the enthusiastic efforts of the man helping her. Why was there no water in Ben's lungs? Surely that was what made people drown? Hannah had seen the same kind of television dramas. Pushing on the chest should clear the water. Then the air could get into the lungs and the victim would splutter and struggle and begin to breathe again. She must be doing something wrong. Hannah pinched Ben's nose more firmly and turned her head. It was becoming harder to drag in the air as her panic increased.

The wail of the approaching siren caused a collective sigh of relief from the spectators. Hannah caught and clutched the sense of hope. People were coming who knew what to do. If anyone could save Ben they were the uniformed officers, laden with lifesaving equipment, now rapidly approaching as the small crowd parted.

Knowledge and skill weren't enough this time. It was too late. No heartfelt cry would reach Ben now but Hannah could feel it being torn from her soul. The sound tried to get past her lips but they were frozen. The cry was trapped. Hannah was trapped. She struggled. Who was holding her back? She had to get free—had to release the scream building inside her—but it was so hard to even breathe.

The sound finally emerged as a groan. The arms holding her became the tangled sheets of her bed. Hannah caught her breath in a painful gasp, turning her face into her pillow as she groaned again. Then she sat up, tightly holding a pillow that was damp from the tears her body had unknowingly shed.

The dream came less frequently now but the horror was never diminished and the aftermath was always the same. The slow trickle of tears. The sense of complete loss. The effect faded a fraction more quickly each time, however, and it only surfaced so painfully in the dream. Resolutely, Hannah pushed back the bedclothes and stood up. The darkness of the hallway did not slow her silent progress. Hannah knew exactly where she was going. She also knew quite well that the loss had not been complete. Just a glance into the cot in the next room was enough to reassure her and to remind her of the joy the birth of Ben's daughter had brought.

It was a joy that had filled the void in her heart and only seemed to get stronger with the passage of time. Hannah had to swallow carefully thanks to the lump that appeared in her throat as she gazed at the tousled blonde curls on the pillow. They framed a small face that appeared to be smiling even in the relaxation of deep sleep. Tiny arms were outstretched, with one hand protruding through the bars of the cot. Hannah was about to touch her daughter's fingers gently when her attention was distracted by a movement behind her. Hannah turned and smiled.

'Morning, Mum.'

'You're up early, love.' Her mother's quiet voice was concerned. 'Is everything all right?'

'Everything's fine,' Hannah assured her. She pointed at the miniature hand escaping the cot. 'I think it might be time to move Heidi into a bed. She's two and half, after all.'

'She loves her cot,' Norma Duncan reminded her daughter. 'And she's still so tiny. I haven't seen her even try to climb out yet.'

'No.' Hannah dismissed the idea and turned away, stifling a yawn. 'I'd better go and have a shower to wake myself up properly.'

'You must be exhausted.' Norma shook her head, following Hannah towards the bathroom. 'You were up till all hours again last night with your nose buried in those books.'

'There's another revision test this morning. And to-morrow we have practical assessments all morning and the written exam in the afternoon. I don't want to fail.'

'You won't.' Norma's smile was confident. 'I've yet to see you fail in anything when you've set your heart on it this much.'

Hannah paused by the bathroom door. 'I'm not so sure about that, Mum.' Her brow furrowed. 'There's ten of us doing this induction course and only six of us are going to get a job.'

'And you'll be one of them,' Norma said firmly. 'You have your shower and I'll get some breakfast ready.'

Hannah let the hot water rinse away the last remnants of the nightmare. She also tried to dismiss the now familiar tension she harboured about the upcoming tests. Her mother was right. She wasn't going to fail. Heidi's birth hadn't been the only major change in her life since Ben's death. Much of the success in her dealing with her own grief had come from discovering what she wanted to do with her life.

Hannah couldn't have saved Ben. Nobody could have. The post-mortem examination had revealed the unsuspected congenital heart defect that had killed him instantaneously. Ben hadn't drowned but Hannah had never forgotten the helplessness of not knowing what to do. Neither had she forgotten the relief and the sense of hope the arrival of the ambulance crew had engendered.

Soon she would be one of them. Maybe she couldn't have saved Ben but Hannah knew, with absolute certainty, that the opportunity to save another life would present itself. Maybe many such opportunities awaited her. She would be ready to try her utmost. If she could be successful, even once, then it would all have been worthwhile. And Hannah had every intention of being successful.

Preferably, a lot more often than once.

CHAPTER TWO

WHY on earth had he chosen that moment to *wink* at her? The effect was quite devastating. Hannah Duncan could feel her cheeks burning uncomfortably as she turned her gaze hurriedly back towards the typewritten sheet lying on the desk in front of her. She could feel the erratic thump of her pulse as she tried to focus on the line of text and a wave of something like despair surfaced as Hannah realised just how shot her concentration now was. The question had seemed so easy only seconds before. Hannah was quite capable of naming the signs and symptoms of a fracture in her sleep. The useful mnemonic was burned into her brain along with the vast array of other information she had spent the last few weeks absorbing so avidly. That useful mnemonic had been felled, along with her concentration, by that totally unexpected wink.

Hannah took a deep breath. She only had to remember the mnemonic and everything would fall back into place. The word was something vaguely mathematical. Catching the fragment of memory gratefully, Hannah felt herself beginning to relax. And there it was. PLUSDISC. She scribbled rapidly. Pain, loss of function, unnatural movement, swelling and shortening, deformity, irregularity, shock and crepitus. Hannah could breathe again. Only one question left and she had learned the principles of fracture management as thoroughly as everything else.

This time, Hannah had no intention of letting her concentration slip. Maybe this was only an informal revision test but the showdown was rapidly approaching. Which four of the people surrounding her in this classroom would be the ones that failed to get the positions they all wanted as probationary ambulance officers? Hannah wasn't going to let anything undermine her chances and that included being flustered by any signs of physical interest in herself. Like that *wink*!

Adam Lewis glanced at the wall clock. He would give the group another five minutes to complete the revision test and then they would fill in the remaining time until lunch by discussing it. He was looking forward to the lunch break. As much as he enjoyed the training and assessment of new recruits to the ambulance service, too much time in the classroom gave him cabin fever.

Adam leaned back in his chair and relaxed a little. Next week he would be back on the road, a paramedic rather than a teacher, the task of sorting the wheat from the chaff of the hopeful recruits over with for several months. These two days left of revision, practical and written assessment were really a formality. Adam Lewis knew quite well already who was going to make the grade from this intake. His glance around the classroom was deceptively idle.

Derek was the oldest of the group at thirty-eight. An ex-policeman, he was an intelligent and quiet man. His physical size was reassuring rather than intimidating. An ideal candidate. Eddie was only twenty-three and rather too shy, but some time on the road would soon cure that. Much of the lad's discomfort came from trying to hide the fact that he was so keen on Hannah. The corner of Adam's mouth twitched sympathetically. He'd have to get over that as well.

Michael sat beside Eddie. He was writing with confidence, probably providing twice as much information as necessary, and would be overly keen to share his answers during discussion time. His mate, Ross, would follow his lead.

Adam's glance flicked over Phil, the taxi driver, who was staring at the ceiling and tapping his pen on the desktop. Phil wasn't going to make it. He was only interested in high drama and the introductory course and period of third crewing over the last few weeks had been enough to demonstrate that trauma work was only a very small percentage of what the job was about. Adam was surprised that Phil had elected to return for the final week of classroom work.

Anne was too nervous to cope and Jackie was more interested in the men than a career. She was watching John, their fitness fanatic, right now instead of working on the test. Adam suppressed an irritated snort and let his gaze move on towards Christine. At thirty-four she was a lot more mature than Jackie but she wasn't any more suited to a career as an ambulance officer, and it wasn't simply personal prejudice due to her family circumstances. Adam Lewis knew what he was doing. Right now, he knew he should be winding up the time spent on the written revision but he couldn't resist adding just another minute. He had deliberately saved his last assessing glance for the pick of the bunch. Hannah Duncan.

She wasn't blushing any longer. Adam wasn't quite sure why he'd smiled and winked at her when he'd caught her momentary lapse in concentration, but the effect of his gesture had been surprising. Did the heightened colour indicate an annoyance at the uninvited attention? Or was Hannah embarrassed by the unprofessional interest in her that her instructor might be advertising? Adam collected himself.

'Time's up,' he announced. 'Let's go over the test and then we can break for lunch.'

As expected, Michael was keen to share his answer on listing the causes of fractures. Adam let him rattle them off, his thoughts straying. Maybe Hannah Duncan didn't realise how interesting she was. She certainly hadn't responded to the overtures from any of the men in the group and she seemed unaware of the way Eddie nearly tripped over himself in his eagerness to partner her in any practical work. Eddie was far too young for Hannah in any case.

Only the other day, Adam had refreshed his knowledge of the information that had appeared on her application form. Hannah was twenty-eight and presumably unmarried, seeing she had listed her mother as next of kin. Previous employment had included a number of jobs overseas, one of them as a technician in a London hospital, and she had, for the last two years, worked as a children's swimming instructor.

'And then there's pathological fractures,' Michael finished. 'From conditions such as bone cancer or osteoporosis.'

'Thanks, Michael.' Adam looked around the class. 'What do we mean by a fracture being caused by an indirect force?'

'The point of impact isn't where the fracture is,' Ross supplied.

'Such as?'

'Landing on your hand and breaking a collar-bone,' Christine said. 'My kids have *all* done that.'

'And?' Adam prompted quickly. He didn't want to get into another discussion centred on Christine's accident-prone offspring. 'Hannah?' Adam's smile was encouraging but impersonal. He didn't want to embarrass or annoy her again.

'Landing on your feet from a height, causing a pelvic or spinal fracture,' Hannah responded quietly.

'Excellent.' Adam's approval was no more than any instructor would have given a capable pupil. 'Let's move on, then. Derek—tell us about limb baselines.'

Hannah watched Derek as he read out the answer he'd prepared. He had done well, dividing his response into both circulation and nervous assessment. As usual, Derek spoke calmly. Quiet but confident. Adam was again nodding approvingly.

'When should we measure the baselines?'

Typically, Adam was ready with a question that would extend the discussion and keep the class focused, but it had been a long morning and Hannah found her attention wandering from fractures and their management. Would Adam notice? And if he did, would he smile at her again…and wink? Or had she simply imagined the quite subtle gesture? The whole group now knew Adam well enough to appreciate his sense of humour and laid-back approach to life. He probably winked at lots of people. Maybe he had a facial twitch which Hannah hadn't previously noticed. No. Hannah knew perfectly well that she had been observing Adam closely enough to familiarise herself with any such physical characteristics.

Hannah's concentration snapped back as she realised the last question had been directed at herself.

'Hypovolaemia,' she responded hurriedly, hoping that she had registered the question correctly, if rather distantly.

'Why?'

'Because some fractures result in a heavy internal blood loss.'

'Which ones in particular?' Adam's intent gaze was still focused on Hannah.

'The pelvis and long bones.'

Adam turned his attention to Jackie. 'What sort of blood loss could you expect from a fractured pelvis?'

Jackie rolled her eyes despairingly and then smiled. 'Um…'

'Three or more litres.' Michael couldn't resist filling the expectant silence. Jackie flashed him a grateful look.

'And how much circulating blood volume does the average adult have?' Adam ignored the byplay.

'Five litres,' Michael added eagerly. 'So three litres represents sixty per cent of circulating volume, which would mean—'

'They're running on empty,' Ross interrupted.

'Exactly.' Adam smoothly took control again. 'Hypovolaemic shock. So, what are some of the other potential complications from fractures?'

Hannah watched as Adam encouraged Eddie to participate in the discussion. Her gaze travelled over Adam's face. Had anyone else noticed that small bump on the bridge of his nose which was probably the result of some childhood mishap? Had the cut that had resulted in the tiny scar dividing his left eyebrow happened at the same time?

'You're quite right, Eddie. Improper management can contribute to both nerve and circulation damage.' Adam was smiling at Eddie widely enough to create the dimples that sometimes appeared above the corners of his mouth.

Now he was listening to Derek go over the complications that contamination could add to fractures. Did Derek appreciate the way Adam's face stilled when he was listening—and the way those dark brown eyes advertised his undivided attention? It certainly made Anne more nervous. The poor girl was stammering as she tried to answer the next question about the consequences of fat emboli.

The discussion was winding up and Hannah glanced at the wall clock. Another few minutes and they would be starting their half-hour lunch-break. Some fresh air might well help her level of concentration. It hadn't been the same ever since that infernal wink. Hannah almost scowled at Adam when she saw him push his dark curls away from his forehead. She hadn't even heard the question Michael had posed, but she recognised Adam's unconscious gesture which indicated that his response required some thought. Yes. Hannah Duncan knew exactly what habits Adam Lewis regularly displayed. And winking was definitely not one of them.

Maybe—perish the thought—Adam was aware of just how closely Hannah had found herself observing him. She dismissed the horrible idea. It wasn't as if the observation had been deliberate or had begun early in their acquaintance. During that introductory course, over a month ago, he had simply been their instructor. His position, as much as his personal manner, commanded attention. And respect. Adam was a paramedic—the top of the scale that this group of would-be trainees aspired to.

The amount of information which had needed to be absorbed had been daunting during that first week, but the intensive training schedule had been scaled down since then to an evening session once a week. The class had been required to accumulate at least sixty hours of road time as a third crew member during the last month, and Hannah had worked hard. She knew that her assessment by the officers she crewed with would carry considerable weight. Unfavourable reviews could undermine any good results from the practical or written examinations.

Perhaps her confidence had grown to a point of allowing herself to relax a little this week, only to find her attention caught as much by her teacher as the guidance he was providing. The depth of her interest had only become obvious when Hannah had found herself distracted from the late night study at home. She was even more conscious of the preoccupation as she lay in bed unable to fall asleep nearly as quickly as usual. Thoughts of Adam Lewis were intruding into her personal life but the intrusion wasn't unpleasant.

It was the first time since Ben's death that Hannah had found herself even remotely interested in a man. A persistent thought had begun in the last few days. *Why not?* Maybe she was ready. Her life was moving on and Hannah had never expected her relationship with her daughter to fulfil all her needs.

Why not, indeed?

'You're looking very thoughtful, Hannah.' Adam didn't wink at her this time. He didn't even smile, but the eyebrow with the tiny scar was raised enough to indicate an alarming appreciation of Hannah's train of thought. The whole class was now looking at her. If Adam queried what she was thinking about then Hannah knew her reaction would be a dead give-away. The blush that the wink had engendered was nothing to what her body was preparing to do this time.

'I'm just hungry,' Hannah said lightly.

The general burst of laughter from the class diffused the attention and Hannah gratefully tidied the books and papers lying on her desk as Adam announced the lunchbreak. Eddie appeared beside Hannah's desk.

'I'm going to the shops to get something to eat,' he told Hannah with overdone casualness. 'Can I get anything for you?'

'No, thanks, Eddie.' Hannah smiled to soften the blow of her refusal. She didn't want to hurt Eddie's feelings but she did wish he would transfer his devotion to someone else. 'I brought mine from home.'

Adam tried not to glare at Eddie, as he sorted through the instructional material on his own desk. He put the overhead projector transparencies he planned to use later to one side. Hannah's simple statement had aroused the intense curiosity that was becoming quite familiar. What was her home like? A smart town house or apartment suited to an active, single lifestyle? He allowed himself one more glance at Hannah as she left the room, accompanied by Derek and Christine, and filed the impression her clothing left.

Faded jeans, leather ankle boots which had seen a fair few miles, a soft cotton shirt with the sleeves rolled up to her elbows and a warm, dark green polar fleece vest that remained casually unzipped. The image was one of comfort and the sense of style it imparted was intrinsic. No. An apartment didn't fit the image any more than an ordinary house in the suburbs. Hannah had a style that was definitely out of the ordinary despite her lack of effort to look smart. Adam felt the corner of his mouth lift a little. Hannah would probably look stylish even in a sack. Or nothing at all...

Adam expelled his breath in an exasperated sigh, turning his attention back to his desk as the classroom emptied. Maybe it was just an advanced case of cabin fever he was suffering from.

Jackie joined Derek and Christine as they sat with Hannah on an outside bench.

'God, that test was awful,' she groaned. 'I hardly got anything right. I'm *never* going to pass the exam tomorrow.' She ripped open the package covering her chocolate bar. 'I hate swotting,' she added fervently.

Derek gave her an amused glance. 'Why do you want to be an ambulance officer, Jackie?'

'I love the uniform.' Jackie grinned around her mouthful of chocolate. 'Blue's my colour. Besides…' she turned her head as John flashed past the small group, off for a quick ride on his racing cycle '…you meet some nice people.'

'What will you do if you don't pass?' Hannah queried, having worried considerably about the issue herself.

Jackie shrugged. 'Try again for another intake, I guess.'

Derek was watching Hannah arrange cheese slices on her crackers. 'What made you want to join the service, Hannah?'

Hannah paused in her task. 'I was once in a situation where someone needed help rather badly,' she said after a short silence. 'And I didn't know what to do.' She fiddled with the cheese slice, sending a crumb tumbling onto the grass. 'When the ambulance crew arrived I envied their assurance in knowing what to do and the ability they had to actually do something to help if it was possible. Unfortunately, in this case, it wasn't.'

'You teach lifesaving to kids, don't you?' Christine joined the conversation. 'Was it a drowning accident that inspired you?'

'Kind of.' Hannah wanted to change the subject. 'What made you decide to apply?'

Christine laughed. 'My boys have been having accidents or getting sick all their lives. I've spent so much time in the emergency department I figured I might as well start getting paid for it.'

'You've got four kids, haven't you?' Jackie was unwrapping her second bar of chocolate. 'Won't the shift work be a hassle?'

'You sound like Adam Lewis,' Christine sighed. 'He's been giving me a hard time about having kids.'

'Really?' Hannah was surprised. 'Why?'

Christine snorted. 'He seems to think that my responsibilities at home will interfere with my ability to do this job. I get the distinct impression that he doesn't approve of working mothers.'

'Oh.' Hannah digested the information. It had been a desire to preserve a degree of privacy which had prevented Hannah mentioning her daughter when the group had shared their early introductions in class. Now she felt relieved that Adam didn't know about Heidi.

'Not that it's any of his business,' Christine continued crossly. 'I've sorted out child care arrangements. Their father can cope in the mornings and when I'm doing nights. That only leaves two days out of eight when they'll need care after school. It'll be a breeze.'

Hannah nodded. The roster was four days on, then four days off. Of the four days on, two were day shifts running from 7 a.m. till 6 p.m. The other two were night shifts covering 6 p.m. to 7 a.m. The long shift hours were preferable because of the four days off they allowed for. Hannah didn't expect to have any difficulty coping. Her mother was only too pleased to help.

Living in a small country town, it had been very lonely for Norma Duncan since Hannah's father had died several years ago. Being an integral part of her daughter's life again had been a godsend for Norma. The addition of a grandchild to help raise had been a bonus, as had been the move to the busy capital city of New Zealand. Norma loved Wellington, despite its well-deserved reputation for having the worst weather in the country.

At the age of fifty-nine, Norma had found a new direction and a new lease on life. Her enthusiasm to meet peo-

ple and put her considerable energy to good use had
prompted her to take a part-time job as a GP's receptionist, but even that commitment wouldn't interfere much
with her determination to be one of Heidi's primary care-
givers. Norma's working hours were confined to mornings, and with the roster system Hannah would be working the need for Heidi to attend the day-care centre would
be only infrequent. Norma had also stated that she would
be more than happy to give up her employment if Heidi
was disadvantaged in any way.

Jackie didn't look as though she shared Hannah's
agreement. 'Having kids is never a breeze,' she declared.
'I'm planning to give it a miss myself. How 'bout you,
Hannah?'

Hannah just smiled. 'I don't think it would be so bad.'
Again, she wanted to change the subject. 'What made you
want to join up, Derek?'

'Same as you,' Derek said thoughtfully. 'As a cop I
was often on a scene like a car accident or an assault or
something well before the ambulance arrived. I didn't like
not being able to help.'

'Didn't you get any first-aid training?'

Derek nodded in response to Hannah's query. 'It wasn't
anything like as detailed as what we've been learning,
though. Just CPR, really. I got to see the AOs carrying
on where I left off.' He grinned. 'I decided I liked the
look of their job more than mine.'

'You've got kids, too, haven't you?' Christine asked.

'Three,' Derek confirmed. 'The youngest is two and the
oldest is ten.'

'I'll bet Adam hasn't asked you whether you'll be able
to cope with the shift work.'

'I've always done shift work,' Derek pointed out. 'The

family's used to it now and Carol, my wife, is delighted about the change in direction.'

Christine shook her head. 'Maybe he's just anti women, then,' she suggested.

Hannah said nothing, concentrating on finishing her lunch. She hadn't had that impression from Adam at all. Quite the contrary, in fact.

The break had refreshed everyone. They gazed at Adam expectantly when he strode through the classroom door at precisely 1 p.m.

'We'll spend most of this afternoon on some practical fracture management work,' he informed them, 'but first I want to run through a revision of spinal injury assessment and management.'

Michael flipped his textbook open to the appropriate chapter as Adam arranged a plastic sheet on the overhead projector screen. Ross and several others followed Michael's example. Phil leaned back in his chair, toying with a ballpoint. Jackie leaned towards John.

'Have you got a pen I could borrow?' she pleaded. 'I seem to have lost mine again.'

'I've got a spare,' Anne offered quickly.

'This should be mostly revision,' Adam said pointedly, 'so you shouldn't need to take notes.' He flicked on the projector and a diagram of a spinal column appeared on the wall. Adam ignored it.

'What's the key consideration in assessing a possible spinal injury?' he queried.

'Neurogenic shock,' Michael answered promptly.

'Pain or paralysis,' Ross added.

Adam's gaze continued around the room. 'Jackie?'

'Paraesthesia,' Jackie suggested triumphantly. 'Or anaesthesia.'

Clearly, the correct answer had not yet been supplied. Anne was Adam's next target. 'What's the first thing that might arouse your suspicion?' he asked patiently.

'Um…' Anne looked worried. 'I guess it's what actually happened.'

'Exactly.' Adam smiled. 'Which is what, Hannah?'

'The mechanism of injury,' Hannah supplied.

'Excellent.' Adam smiled at her warmly. Hannah dropped her gaze, uncomfortable with the thought that she was getting the credit for the correct answer when it had, in fact, been Anne who had known that it wasn't just the signs and symptoms of spinal injury that needed consideration. Adam didn't pause. 'What are some of the mechanisms?'

'Compression,' Michael responded. 'A jump or fall from a height or being hit by a falling object.'

'Good.' Adam nodded. 'What else?'

'Penetration.' Phil leaned forward in his chair, suddenly interested. 'Gunshot or stabbing injuries.'

'Distraction.' Jackie was peering over John's shoulder at his textbook.

'From hangings,' Phil added with relish.

Anne groaned faintly. 'Oh, yuk.'

Adam waited until they had exhausted all the possibilities. 'Why is the MOI so important?'

'Because the patient might be unconscious,' Derek said. 'They might not be able to tell you about any symptoms.'

'Could they have a spinal injury and not have any signs or symptoms?'

The class was silent. Some began nodding and Adam looked at them approvingly.

'I attended a traffic accident recently,' he said conversationally. 'Car versus tree. Only one patient and he was standing in front of the car by the time we arrived on the scene. He was rather upset about the damage to his vehicle. It was a company car and he wasn't insured to drive it so he was going to have to foot the panelbeating bill himself.' Adam stroked his chin thoughtfully. 'He insisted there was nothing at all wrong with him physically and he refused examination or transport to hospital, but I persisted in trying to change his mind because I'd noticed that he rubbed his neck occasionally while he was talking. Eventually, I persuaded him to let me put a collar on just in case and take him into Emergency for a check-up.'

The class was listening intently.

'Turned out he had an undisplaced fracture of C2,3,' Adam finished calmly. 'If he'd turned his head or coughed he might have had a lot more than the insurance to worry about. He would probably have been a tetraplegic for the rest of his life.'

The class was suitably impressed. The impact of Adam's story was cut short, however, by the unexpected and strident notes of an electronic tune. The opening bars of the 'William Tell' overture were coming from Christine's cellphone. She looked embarrassed as she fished it out from her bag. Adam looked annoyed.

'Oh, God!' Christine exclaimed seconds later. 'How bad is it?' She screwed her face into a pained expression. '*Where* did you say he was bleeding from?'

The class exchanged amused glances, apart from Hannah who was watching Adam. He, in turn, had Christine fixed with his intent, listening-mode gaze. His face was still expressionless as he watched Christine end the call.

'I'm going to have to go,' she apologised. 'Robbie's fallen off the bike shed roof and they want me to collect him from school.'

Adam was frowning now. His expression could have

been one of concern for Christine's youngest son but his words dispelled the notion.

'What would you do if this happened when you were out on a shift?' he queried coolly.

Christine was hurriedly collecting her belongings. 'I don't know,' she admitted distractedly. 'I thought I had everything worked out.'

'Give it some thought,' Adam directed. Christine was now halfway to the door. 'We might need to have a chat tomorrow.'

The class exchanged glances again but they weren't amused this time. Hannah stared at her desk. It was obvious that Christine had an extra obstacle in this competition and she had probably just wiped out any chance of success. Was Adam being too hard on Christine or was his concern that her parental responsibilities would interfere with her ability to work justified? What would happen if he found out about Heidi? Hannah tried to dismiss the alarming thought. He wasn't going to find out—not before tomorrow, anyway. Hannah would never be faced with the awkward situation Christine was dealing with at present in any case. Even in an emergency Hannah knew she could entrust Heidi's care, at least temporarily, to her doting grandmother.

The atmosphere was a little subdued after Christine left. Adam pushed his fingers through his hair, collecting his thoughts, then moved decisively. He switched the projector off, collected a large bag from the corner of the room and unzipped it to remove the contents.

'Stiffneck collars,' he observed, fanning them out in his hands. 'Who's put one on in the field so far?'

'I have,' Michael said eagerly.

'So have I.' Anne sounded more tentative.

'Any problems?'

'Nope.' Michael sounded pleased. 'I remembered how to size and pre-form it.'

'Anne?' Adam coaxed.

'I found it really difficult,' Anne admitted. 'This woman had long hair and it got all caught up in the Velcro. She wasn't very happy with me and it made me feel more nervous.'

Adam nodded. 'It's quite different doing something for real even after you've practised it endlessly in the class-room.' He smiled reassuringly at Anne. 'Something you haven't catered for, like long hair or big earrings, can really throw you.' Moving to reposition a chair, Adam glanced casually sideways.

'Come and sit here, Hannah,' he invited. 'You don't mind undoing your hair for a minute, do you?'

Hannah shook her head. Anne's hair was short, Jackie's blonde bob only shoulder length. She was the obvious choice if Adam wanted to demonstrate coping with long hair. Hannah pulled the band from the end of her plait and unbraided her thick hair by raking her fingers through it as she sat down facing the class.

'Come and choose a collar, Anne.' Adam fluffed out Hannah's hair so that it fell around her shoulders. 'We need two people for this job,' he reminded the class.

Eddie stood up so fast that his chair tipped over. His face was bright red as he joined the others at the front of the classroom.

'You hold Hannah's head in a neutral position,' Adam directed Eddie, 'and Anne can put the collar on.'

Hannah could feel the tremble in Eddie's fingers as they held the sides of her head. Anne put the chinpiece of the collar on Hannah's chest and then slid it up into position under her chin. Hannah's hair immediately got in the way. Adam let them struggle only briefly before taking over

Eddie's part. At a little over six feet in height, Adam was
a whole head taller than Eddie. He was also considerably
broader and Hannah could feel the deep reverberation of
his voice as her skull rested lightly against his chest.

'OK, I'm holding the head in the neutral position,' he
stated. 'Anne's going to size the collar and then hold it
in place ready to apply it.'

Hannah sat very still. She could feel every single one
of Adam's fingers as they cradled her skull. Eddie's hands
had been simply support. Adam's felt as if they were giving off an energy that travelled right through her body.

'As soon as the chinpiece is giving some support, I'm
going to move this hand,' Adam explained. 'I'll get the
hair out of Anne's way.' His fingers brushed Hannah's
neck as he scooped the tresses aside. 'Now Anne can fit
the collar and tighten it.'

Adam released Hannah's hair and watched it ripple
over the hard plastic of the collar. He had known all along
just how soft that glorious silver hair would be, but the
sensation of having it run through his fingers was extraor-
dinary. Adam went onto autopilot as he set the class to
practise their management of spinal fractures. Soon they
were all busily fitting collars to each other and using back-
boards and scoop stretchers to refresh the techniques of
total spinal immobilisation. Adam provided direction and
supervision. He watched over them all. He watched
Hannah in particular.

Adam suppressed the urge to sigh. This preoccupation
was becoming far too noticeable to ignore any longer.
Hannah hadn't bothered to rebraid her hair. She had
drawn it back into a tidy ponytail, but it became looser
as she worked and small tendrils escaped to frame her
face. Why hadn't Adam noticed earlier that the ash blonde
of her unusual hair colour was reflected in those soft grey

eyes? The answer was that, quite properly, Adam's interest in Hannah had been purely professional up until a very short time ago.

She had caught his attention during that introductory course due to her sheer eagerness and the ability to succeed which she displayed. Adam had to admit that he was tougher on the women applying for this job. The service was male dominated for good reason. The job was demanding—physically, mentally and emotionally. It could be downright dangerous at times. The women who succeeded were special. They were highly motivated and very intelligent. They required both a physical and emotional strength that made them stand out.

Hannah stood out, all right. It had been a very long time since Adam had found himself quite so interested in a woman. When this selection process was completed, and he became her colleague rather than her instructor and assessor, maybe he would test the water and see what her response might be.

Why not?

Michael thought Adam's smile was showing approval of his strapping technique but Adam knew differently.

Why not, indeed?

CHAPTER THREE

HANNAH'S body was disobeying commands.

Her legs should have carried her body away some time ago, when Michael and Ross had decided to head for home. Her limbs had ignored the much earlier opportunity when John had declined another mineral water and left the gathering. Now they were reluctant to co-operate when Derek excused himself.

'I'll take you home, Eddie,' Derek said casually.

'That's OK.' Eddie shook his head. 'I was planning to give Hannah a lift.'

'You're not driving anywhere.' Derek's tone was kind but firm. 'I'm not an ex-cop for nothing.'

Eddie flushed and deposited his empty beer glass with the sizable collection that littered the table. 'We *were* celebrating,' he mumbled.

'We sure were.' Derek grinned. 'We passed.'

'Indeed you did.' Adam nodded with satisfaction. 'You've all done well. Eddie, I'm sure your ability to make good judgements will inspire you to accept Derek's offer.'

'I've got my own car anyway, Eddie,' Hannah added. 'I'll be driving myself home in a minute.'

Eddie looked despondent but then straightened his shoulders. 'I guess I'll see you next week, anyway, Hannah.' A proud smile escaped. 'At work.'

'Bound to,' Hannah agreed. 'Except I don't think we're on the same team, are we? I've been assigned to Blue shift.'

Eddie's shoulders slumped again. 'I'm Red,' he said sadly. 'Maybe I could swap.'

'Sorry.' Adam didn't sound the least bit apologetic. 'Not possible, I'm afraid, Eddie. You'll be on your assigned shifts for your three-month probation period. Sometimes things get shuffled after you pass your Grade 1 qualification. Depends on how well you do.'

'I'll do my best,' Eddie responded earnestly. 'I plan to go places.' He hiccuped loudly and looked embarrassed again, his face matching the reddish tinge of his hair.

'Home is the only place you're going right now.' Derek put an arm around Eddie's shoulders and steered him towards the door.

Adam shook his head and smiled ruefully. 'He's keen.'

'So am I.' Hannah had to laugh at Adam's astonished expression. 'I didn't mean on Eddie. I was talking about the *job*.'

'You'll do very well,' Adam said seriously. 'If anyone's going places, it'll be you.'

Hannah lowered her gaze modestly. Now was the time to thank her instructor and follow the example of her classmates by leaving their celebratory gathering. Her legs didn't even twitch.

'I did feel sorry for Anne and Jackie. They were very disappointed not to pass.'

'They can always try again.' Adam didn't sound particularly sympathetic. 'Anne needs to build her confidence and Jackie, well, she just needs to grow up a bit.'

'Christine must have been disappointed, too. She was very keen.'

Adam shrugged. 'It was her decision to pull out. She's going to wait until her children are a bit older.'

'And Phil didn't even show up for the exam.' Hannah shook her head in bewilderment, then smiled shyly. 'Do you know, I rushed home and put my uniform on to show off to my mother? I felt absurdly proud of myself.'

'So you should. You topped the class in those tests.' Adam still sounded solemn. 'Congratulations.'

'Thanks.' Hannah found it astonishingly difficult to break the eye contact they held. Finally her legs obeyed her command and she rose hurriedly. 'I'd better go,' she excused herself. 'It's getting pretty late.'

'Indeed.' Adam also stood up. It *was* late. They were the last patrons left in the small pub. The staff were busy with dishwashers in the kitchen and the sound of glassware being sorted carried through to punctuate the short silence that fell. Hannah had been sitting in the corner and Adam was now blocking her exit. Neither of them moved.

'I'm looking forward to Monday,' Adam said softly.

'Me, too.' Hannah tried to curb her excitement but it wasn't easy. 'I start work,' she added.

'I know.' Adam was watching Hannah carefully. 'I'm on Blue shift as well. We'll probably be working together.' Adam knew perfectly well that they would be crewed together. He'd made it his business to organise the first shifts for the new intake himself.

'Oh.' Hannah caught her bottom lip between her teeth.

'You look disappointed,' Adam teased.

'No, it's not that,' Hannah said quickly. Adam was standing too close to her. Being in the same room was too close right now. She needed to move before she revealed more than she'd intended to. This time her body moved without any conscious command but Adam failed to give way. They were almost touching. 'I...uh...' Hannah stumbled, then trailed off into silence.

'It's quite possible to maintain a professional working relationship quite apart from how well we get to know each other outside working hours.' Adam's intent gaze was locked onto Hannah's. 'I would rather like to get to know you, Hannah Duncan.'

Adam's face was even closer than his body as he leaned forward. If Hannah moved even fractionally, it would only be considered an invitation to be kissed. She felt her head tilting and then closed her eyes at the feather-light touch of Adam's lips on her own. It was gone almost instantly and Hannah opened her eyes to find Adam smiling at her.

'I'm not sure I can wait until Monday,' he murmured. 'Would you come out with me tomorrow night?'

'Do you really think that's a good idea?' Hannah asked slowly. The potential complications of a personal relationship with a colleague presented themselves with lightning speed. The coalescence of a week's preoccupation with the attractions of Adam Lewis was doing its best to override them.

'I think—' Adam's face was looming closer again as he spoke very quietly '—That it's quite possibly the best idea I've ever had.'

Agreeing to Adam's invitation had quite possibly been the best decision Hannah had ever made. The thought of seeing him again on Monday morning vied successfully with the excitement of officially donning her full uniform for the first time. Hannah eyed her reflection with a glow of satisfaction. The crisp, white open-necked shirt had navy blue epaulettes with AMBULANCE embroidered in red. Tailored, navy blue trousers covered the tops of the stout, black, lace-up boots. Hannah slotted a pen into the front pocket of her shirt and attached the pair of shears, a penlight torch and small glove pouch to her leather belt. She grinned at her reflection. Armed, but hopefully not dangerous.

It was only 6 a.m. but Hannah couldn't wait any longer.

She stole into Heidi's bedroom and kissed her daughter softly. The small girl stirred and smiled in her sleep, giving Hannah a sharp twinge of regret. Was she doing the right thing in taking on a career that would mean so much time away from her young child?

Norma was wrapping her dressing gown around herself as she emerged from the bedroom on the other side of Heidi's.

'All set, love?' She peered at Hannah's face in the dim light of the hallway and then smiled understandingly. 'Don't worry. Heidi will be just fine. She loves day care and when I pick her up at lunchtime we're going to have a picnic in the park and see if we can find any ducklings to feed yet.'

'It should be me taking her to the park,' Hannah said quietly. 'I've been so excited about getting this job that I didn't really think about how guilty I would feel when it came to the crunch.'

'You've been excited because you know it's exactly what you want to do. You need a life, too, Hannah. You've got too much to offer to shut yourself away with just Heidi and me. Besides, it gives me some time alone with my granddaughter and you know what it means to me to be such an important part of her life.'

Hannah hugged her mother. 'I couldn't do any of this without you.'

'I suspect you're doing more for me.' Norma smiled. 'I haven't felt this alive or needed since you were tiny. You never know, you might do the same for your daughter one day.' Norma returned the hug with affection. 'Though not under the same circumstances, I hope.' She released Hannah. 'Now, have you had some breakfast?'

'I couldn't eat a thing, Mum. I'm way too nervous.'

'You'll be fine.' Norma watched Hannah collect her

uniform jersey and waterproof jacket from the hanger near the front door. 'Do you know who you'll be working with today?'

'Um…Adam, I think.' Hannah fiddled with her car keys.

'Oh!' Norma's eyebrows lifted. 'Is this the same Adam who kept you up till all hours on Saturday night?'

'Mmm.' Hannah pulled the door open. 'I'd better go, Mum. Wish me luck.'

'I'm not sure I need to.' Norma's smile turned into a grin. 'You seem to be doing rather well all by yourself.'

Her mother didn't know the half of it. Hannah pulled into one of the assigned parking slots for day shift crews and eyed the Jeep parked beside her. The distinctive vehicle belonged to Adam. His taste in things a little out of the ordinary had extended to property as well, and Hannah had been impressed by his house when he'd taken her home after their dinner date.

Tucked into the hills above Oriental Bay, the picture windows and terrace had afforded a spectacular view over the inner city and harbour. They had watched the inter-island ferry cruise majestically towards Aotea Quay as daylight faded and the lights of the city began to compete for attention.

Not that they had stayed on the terrace for that long. It was the fact that Adam hadn't exactly kept her *up* till all hours on Saturday night that now made Hannah feel extremely uncomfortable. She hadn't expected they would get to know each other quite so well on a first date. She wouldn't have believed how right it had seemed or how…perfect it had been to make love with him. How could she possibly work professionally with a man who had moved from mentor to lover with such graceful ease?

The worry was forgotten the moment Hannah entered the garage. Adam was standing in front of a parked ambulance.

'Grab a life pack, will you, Hannah? There's a priority-one call waiting and we're the only crew on station right now.'

Hannah ran to the storeroom. She remembered to clip fresh batteries into the life pack and check the supply of electrodes. Adam had the engine running as she climbed into the passenger seat of the ambulance.

'Just put it on the floor for now.' Adam pushed the responding button on the radio console and pulled out of the garage. He flicked the beacons on and Hannah could see the flashing red and blue lights reflected in the windows of the building as they shot down the driveway. The barrier arm lifted automatically and Adam turned on the siren as they entered the early morning traffic.

'It's number 26, Riverside Drive,' he called over the noise of the siren. 'Check the map and tell me what the most direct route is.'

Hannah clamped her feet around the life pack and reached for the laminated street-map folder. She flicked through the index pages.

'I think it comes off Clarence Road,' Adam shouted. 'In Karori. Have you found it yet?'

'No.' Hannah had only just found the page number. She glanced up as they swerved to find they were now travelling on the wrong side of the road, clearing a line of traffic waiting at a red light. Adam changed the siren tone to a shorter yelp as they approached the intersection and Hannah returned her gaze to the map index, finding that she had now forgotten the grid reference. She fought a wave of panic. Her first task and she was failing already!

Seconds later, she gave a relieved cry. 'I've found it! Where are we now?'

'Clarence Road.'

'OK—it's the third on the right. Number 26 should be at this end.'

Adam turned off the siren as they turned into Riverside Drive. He pushed the 'located' indicator on the transmitter and switched off the beacons and engine at the same time. 'This is a chest pain,' he informed Hannah. 'Grab the portable oxygen and the life pack. I'll take my kit.' Adam picked up the large toolkit-style box. The kit contained an astonishing array of supplies, including equipment to intubate and ventilate a patient, IV cannulae and fluids and the full range of drugs that paramedics were qualified to administer.

The front door of the house was ajar. Adam knocked but didn't pause. 'It's the ambulance,' he called.

'In here.' The voice came from the back of the house.

Adam glanced at Hannah. 'You can do this assessment if you like.'

Hannah went ahead of Adam into a kitchen to find a man sitting at the table. His face was grey and he had a hand pressed to the centre of his chest.

'Hello, sir.' Hannah hoped she didn't sound as nervous as she felt. 'My name's Hannah. Can you tell me what the problem is?'

'Pain,' the man told her succinctly. 'Just here.' He moved his hand towards his throat. 'And here.'

'Can you describe what this pain is like?'

'It's like a ten-ton truck…sitting on my chest.' The patient gasped for air mid-sentence.

Hannah noticed the small red canister of Nitrolingual spray on the table beside them. 'Do you have a history of heart problems, sir?'

The man nodded. 'Heart attack two years ago. Angina since then but never as...bad as this.'

Hannah was desperately trying to remember all the things she should ask. 'Has the GTN spray made any difference to the pain?'

'Only for a while. It's worse than ever now.'

Hannah took a deep breath. 'On a scale of zero to ten, with zero being no pain and ten being the worst pain you've ever experienced, what score would you give this?' She could see Adam unwrapping an oxygen mask. Damn. She should have done that herself while she was asking the questions.

'Nine,' the man groaned. 'No, make that ten.'

'When did it start?'

'About half an hour ago.'

'And were you aware of any other symptoms at that time?'

'I felt sick...' The patient moved his hand to cover his eyes. 'And I started sweating.'

He was still sweating profusely. He didn't look at all well. Hannah knew they had only been in the room for a couple of minutes but she felt they should be doing a lot more than just asking questions. Could she move on or had she left out something important?

'Could you pop some electrodes on, please, Hannah?' Adam suggested calmly. He fitted the oxygen mask on their patient. 'How long ago did you use your spray?' he queried.

'Just before you arrived.'

Adam picked up the yellow card lying beside the spray canister. 'Does this list your current medications, Mr Crombie?'

Hannah was uncurling the electrode wires which were determined to remain tangled. Why hadn't she thought of checking the standard medication card most patients used to learn the name of their patient? Not to mention what drugs he was on. And she had forgotten to introduce Adam. There were just too many things to try and remember at the same time.

'I'm just going to stick these patches on you, Mr Crombie,' Hannah explained, 'so we can see how your heart's behaving at the moment.' She concentrated on her task. White went on right. She peeled the backing off the electrode and positioned it under the right collar-bone. Black went on left and the red electrode went on the left-hand side below the level of the umbilicus. Hannah turned on the life pack.

Adam was opening his kit. 'I'm going to put a small needle in your hand, Mr Crombie,' Adam told their patient. 'We'll be able to give you something to help the pain then. Hannah, could you take a blood pressure, please?'

'Sure.' Hannah reached for the cuff and stethoscope, glad of the directed task. She moved so that she and Adam had separate arms to work on.

'Have you checked the rhythm we've got?' Adam's tone was deceptively casual as Hannah glanced at the life-pack screen. It was far from normal. The trace looked like a child's scribbled attempt to draw a mountain range.

'Do you know what it is?' Adam queried.

Hannah bit her lip. Was it ventricular tachycardia or fibrillation? Neither were good but fibrillation was only a step away from arresting completely. The trace was too formed and regular to be fibrillation—yet.

'Is it VT?'

Adam nodded briefly. 'I'm going to give him some lignocaine as well as the morphine.' He gave their patient an assessing glance. 'How are you feeling right now, Mr Crombie?'

'Not the best.'

'Are you feeling faint at all?'

'I do feel a bit dizzy.'

'BP's ninety-five over sixty,' Hannah reported. She had taken it twice to make sure. No wonder he was feeling dizzy. 'Shall I bring a stretcher in?'

'Thanks.' Adam was injecting medication into the in-travenous line he had inserted.

Hannah had a struggle getting the stretcher out of the back of the ambulance single-handed. She recognised the value of the heavy boots she was wearing, having dropped a wheel directly onto her toes. By the time she pushed the bed into Mr Crombie's kitchen, she found that Adam had administered another dose of lignocaine and the ECG trace was settling into a more normal pattern, with only the occasional extra beat. The potential to deteriorate was still high and Hannah sensed that Adam was keen to transport their patient as quickly as possible. She followed directions rapidly as they positioned Mr Crombie on the stretcher, tidied and packed up the equipment and loaded everything back into the ambulance.

Hannah sat in the back, monitoring their patient's condition on the ride to hospital and doing her best to fill in all the paperwork correctly. Adam still found a lot of gaps when he checked later. Mr Crombie's care had now been taken over by the emergency department staff.

'You need to attach a segment of the ECG trace on the back here,' Adam told Hannah. He pulled the strip of paper through his fingers. 'Do you recognise the abnormalities?'

'I'm not sure,' Hannah confessed.

'Well, there's obvious ST elevation. See?' Adam

tapped the trace with his ballpoint pen. 'The T-wave is inverted and there's Q-wave formation. The T and Q wave changes are probably left over from his previous heart attack but the ST segment elevation is a clear sign of a new event.'

Hannah studied the trace while Adam filled in the drugs that had been administered and signed the form. He carried on his check.

'You need to put how many litres of oxygen he was on here,' Adam pointed out.

Hannah wrote in the figure ten.

'And the gauge size of the IV cannula goes in here.'

'Was it eighteen?'

'No, sixteen.' Adam pointed to a row of boxes at the top of the form. 'Did you get the times through on your pager?'

Hannah groaned. 'I forgot to even put my pager on. Sorry.'

'Don't apologise. You've done very well.' Adam unclipped his own pager from his belt and scrolled the information available. He rapidly filled in the times they had been dispatched, had located and then left the scene and their arrival time at the hospital. Then he smiled at Hannah. 'It's now 7 a.m.,' he told her, 'and you are officially starting your new job as of now. Good morning,' he said belatedly. He lowered his voice. 'I must say it's *very* nice to see you again, Hannah.'

Hannah smiled back but averted her gaze from Adam quickly. It was as though a switch had been thrown. While working on the job she had completely forgotten she had anything other than a professional relationship with her senior colleague. Now she was far too aware of the personal side. If only she could switch it off just as easily when they were dispatched again, maybe this would be easier than she had anticipated.

'We might get time for a coffee before the next call,' Adam suggested hopefully. His pager beeped as he finished speaking and he smiled ruefully. 'Spoke too soon, didn't I?' He read the message. 'Another priority-one call,' he told Hannah. 'Breathing difficulties. Let's go.' He was already propelling the freshly made-up stretcher towards the automatic doors. Hannah ran to catch up.

Their patient turned out to be a woman of about Hannah's age who had been hyperventilating for some time. Adam persuaded her to slow her breathing down and her symptoms gradually subsided.

'I thought my hands were paralysed,' she told them apologetically. 'And my lips went all numb.'

'How are you feeling now?' Adam queried.

'Silly,' she said with embarrassment. 'We shouldn't have called you but Joe panicked a bit, I think.'

The woman's husband had been watching anxiously. Now he scowled at his wife. 'It was you that got yourself all worked up into a state,' he snapped.

The small, pyjama-clad child in the man's arms promptly burst into tears and wriggled free to run towards his mother. She pulled the boy onto her lap.

'It's all right, sweetie,' she soothed. 'Mummy's fine now.'

'Yes, but for how long?' The husband shook his head in disgust. 'Cath's starting a new job today,' he told Adam and Hannah. 'She doesn't seem to think she's going to cope.'

Hannah smiled sympathetically at their patient. She knew what that sort of nervous anticipation was like.

'It's not the job, Joe. I'm worried about leaving Peter in day care. As you well know,' she added accusingly.

She sent an appealing glance towards Adam. 'He's going to hate it.'

Adam made a noncommittal sound, turning quickly back to the paperwork he was completing.

'And you know we can't afford the mortgage if you don't go back to work.' Joe's voice rose angrily. 'It wasn't *my* idea for you to get pregnant.'

The child's wails rose at the tone of his father's voice. Hannah could sense the tension in Adam's controlled movements and words.

'I need you to sign this form, Mrs Harvey,' he said. 'It states that we attended your call and that transportation to hospital was not required.'

When the form was signed, Adam signalled their departure.

'I'm really sorry,' the woman said again, 'but it wasn't *my* idea to call you.'

Hannah followed Adam out of the house. She could hear the voices rising behind them.

'And I suppose it wasn't your bloody idea to get pregnant either?'

'I didn't exactly do it by myself.' Cath sounded furious. 'For God's sake, Joe—can't you see how much you're upsetting Peter with your shouting?'

Adam shut the front door firmly, muting the child's wails. 'Happy families,' he muttered.

Hannah climbed into the front seat of the ambulance. 'It can be difficult,' she offered. 'Juggling motherhood with a career.'

'I wouldn't know,' Adam said grimly. 'And I certainly have no intention of finding out. Imagine living with that every morning?' He unhooked the microphone from the dashboard. 'Unit 241 to Control.'

'Go ahead, 241.' The response was immediate.

'Transportation not required,' Adam informed the control room. 'We're available in Cranford Crescent.'

'Roger. Return available, 241.'

'Good.' Adam returned the microphone to its clip. 'Maybe we'll get that coffee now.'

Hannah watched the build-up of the rush-hour traffic as they drove back towards headquarters, situated in the central city suburb of Newtown, not far from the main hospital complex. So Adam had no intention of finding out about the logistics of life with a working mother. What would he say now if he found out about Heidi?

Hannah had no intention of trying to hide the most important part of her life but did she want to give up the new excitement of the rapport she had discovered with Adam? The answer to that was resoundingly negative. Hannah tried to ignore the tense internal knot she could feel forming. Maybe Adam just didn't like Monday mornings. Or noisy children. Or being drawn into a marital dispute. There was so much she had yet to learn about m. It seemed quite reasonable that he still had a lot to rn about her as well. Including the fact that she was a king mother.

Hannah was exhausted by the end of her first shift. Being double-crewed was very different to having been out on the road as a third crew member and observer. People expected her to perform and Hannah felt the weight of the responsibility and capability her uniform implied. The day had been a busy one with the only downtime at headquarters being a half-hour lunch-break. The calls had been many and varied.

Hannah had made what seemed like a huge number of minor errors, had had trouble with the paperwork and had fumbled some even basic tasks like the occasion when she had forgotten to turn on the main oxygen cylinder until they'd been halfway back to the hospital. Adam had been very patient. His coaching and encouragement left Hannah feeling that she would, one day, be very good at this job.

'Come out for a drink,' Adam invited as their shift ended and they completed their task of washing down the ambulance. 'Let's celebrate you surviving your first shift.'

'I can't,' Hannah apologised. 'Not tonight.' She couldn't wait to get home and reassure herself that her mother and Heidi had enjoyed their day.

'Got another date, then?' Adam's tone was deceptively light.

'Of course not.' Hannah frowned. Did Adam think she would have more than one man in her life at the same time? 'I told you I wasn't in a relationship.'

'Just checking.' Adam's smile was almost tentative. 'You gave me a fright, that's all.' He leaned forward to take the bucket and mop from Hannah's hands. 'I'd hate to think that Saturday night was an experience you had no desire to repeat.'

Hannah's breath caught. The desire for a repetition was strong enough to strangle her right then. It was difficult to say anything.

'I'm…uh…just tired,' she managed. 'And it's another early start tomorrow.'

'I'm first call tomorrow,' Adam told her. 'You'll be crewed with Tom, I expect.'

'Oh.' Hannah couldn't hide her disappointment.

Adam's smile was much more confident this time. 'Perhaps we should make a date for the end of the week,' he suggested softly.

Hannah swallowed hard. 'I think that's a very good idea.'

'So do I.' Adam leaned a little closer. He didn't quite

touch Hannah but she could feel his body quite well enough to raise a fresh and overwhelming wave of desire.

'I think,' Adam whispered carefully, 'that it's probably the second-best idea I've ever had.'

'What was the first?' Hannah teased.

'Last Saturday night, of course.'

The smile they shared acknowledged the redundancy of Hannah's question. It also promised a repetition that would in no way diminish their memory of their first time together.

It didn't. Both Adam and Hannah recognised the significance of the relationship they had begun by the second evening they spent together at Adam's house. By the following Saturday it seemed as though Hannah's life was settling into a new and very exciting pattern. There were three distinct components—home, work…and Adam.

Home was no problem. Heidi barely noticed the extra time Hannah was absent. If she did, it was more than compensated for by the efforts Hannah made to ensure the time they did have together was special. Work was becoming much more manageable. By the end of her third series of shifts, Hannah was familiar with most of the equipment and protocols. She had gained a reputation with all the members of Blue shift as being a fast learner, more competent than most people at her stage of training and a willing and cheerful colleague.

Derek, the ex-policeman from Hannah's intake, had also joined Blue shift. He, too, was proving popular with their workmates. When Derek and Hannah compared notes after three weeks, they agreed that they were loving the job and it was becoming easier as they got used to it.

Hannah was nowhere near being used to being in love again. The heightened awareness and pleasure she was taking in all aspects of life was constant. She had only crewed with Adam once since her first day but their paths often crossed during their shifts. They might be in the emergency department at the same time, delivering patients, or at headquarters for a meal break. On night shifts there were frequently long, quiet spells with plenty of time to talk quietly over a coffee. After midnight, staff on duty were allowed to sleep if the workload allowed. There were several small bedrooms on a mezzanine floor above the garage. Hannah and Adam rarely made use of them.

Surprisingly, it had been easy, so far, to keep their relationship private. Hannah got on well with everybody and if Adam appeared to enjoy her company it wasn't enough to raise any eyebrows. Hannah didn't question any reason Adam might have to separate his professional and private lives. She was doing exactly the same thing herself to an even greater degree, having two components to her private life. The distinction made things a lot easier at work and perhaps Adam felt the same way Hannah did— that what they had was too new and too precious to share with anybody else just yet.

The one person who couldn't fail to know precisely what was going on was Norma. She sat beside her daughter on the Sunday afternoon at the end of Hannah's third week as an ambulance officer. Having been on duty the night before, Hannah had slept until nearly 2 p.m. The sunny and unusually still weather had enticed them all out for a walk, and now Hannah and Norma were keeping a watchful eye on Heidi as she explored the adventure playground in the botanical gardens.

'You're looking happier than I think I've ever seen you look, love,' Norma told her daughter.

'I am happy, Mum.' Hannah gave her mother a wistful smile. 'I'm almost afraid of it.'

'Why?'

'Because it feels too good to be true. It can't last.'

'Of course it can. It might even get better.'

'You think so?' Hannah caught her bottom lip between her teeth but a smile broke through. 'I'd be more than happy if things just stayed the way they are.'

'It's not just the job, is it?'

'No.' Hannah turned her gaze towards her own daughter. Heidi was coming towards her, a tiny dungaree-clad figure, wearing a sun hat and a large smile.

'Look, Mumma!'

'I see, darling.' Hannah accepted the offering. 'It's a leaf. Isn't it pretty?' She bent forward to kiss Heidi's curls. 'See if you can find me another one.'

Norma watched her granddaughter toddle off purposefully towards the hedge behind the jungle gym.

'So, when am I going to meet this Adam?'

'I don't know, Mum.' Hannah's face clouded. 'It's a bit tricky.'

Norma gave Hannah a startled glance. 'Why is that?'

Hannah sighed. 'He doesn't know about Heidi.'

'Oh.' Norma was silent for a moment. 'Is there any particular reason why you haven't told him?'

'Mmm.' Hannah was reluctant to explore the subject but she couldn't push it away for ever. And who better to discuss it with than her mother? 'You remember I told you about Christine? She was convinced that Adam didn't approve of working mothers—that he thought their commitments at home would interfere with being able to do the job well. That's why I never told anyone. I thought it might jeopardise my chances of becoming an ambulance officer.'

'You've got the job now,' Norma reminded her.

'I know.' Hannah chewed her bottom lip worriedly. 'But now there's another reason not to tell him.'

'Which is?'

'He hates kids.'

'Did *he* tell you that?' Norma asked incredulously.

'Not exactly, but Tom did. I attended a car accident one day when I was on with Tom. Adam backed us up in case we needed a paramedic. The mother needed to go to hospital. She wasn't seriously injured but Adam refused to take the children with her. There was a little girl about Heidi's age who was really upset at being separated from her mother so I asked Tom why they couldn't have travelled together. Tom said that Adam hates kids. It's kind of a joke around headquarters.'

Norma had listened to the story with a frown. 'And you believe it?'

'I'm not sure,' Hannah admitted. 'There *were* three children so it was too many to take in one ambulance. But there's been other things as well.'

'Such as?'

Hannah thought of the call to the worried mother about to start a new job and leave her son at day care. She remembered Adam's grim appraisal of their family life together. She shrugged. 'Oh, I don't know, Mum. It's a feeling, really. He jokes a lot and calls children rug rats and ankle-biters. And he always makes a show of dreading paediatric calls. If he doesn't really hate children then he makes a good show of pretending.'

Heidi was returning, her small fists clutching a handful of leaves. She beamed at the two women.

'Look, Nanna! Look, Mumma! Lotsa leaf.'

Hannah gathered her daughter onto her lap. 'Would you like a swing before we go home, darling?'

'Yes!' The leaves scattered as Heidi excitedly slid down from her mother's lap. 'Swing *now*!'

Norma caught Hannah's eye. 'Do you want this relationship with Adam to go anywhere?'

Hannah ignored the insistent tugging on her hand. 'Yes, I do, Mum. Very much. That's why I'm scared to say anything that might change things.'

Hannah walked the short distance to the swings and lifted Heidi into the bucket seat. The small girl crowed with delight at the first gentle push. Hannah was aware that her mother had come to stand beside her but she kept her eyes on her task. She caught the swing and pushed it again.

'I never thought I could feel like this again, Mum. Maybe my memories have faded a bit but it feels like it's even more than I ever had with Ben. A lot more.' Hannah was nodding as she gave her mother a quick glance, having pushed the swing away again.

Norma looked rather serious. 'You'll have to tell him the truth some time.'

'I'm working on it.'

'Doesn't he wonder why you haven't invited him home?'

Hannah grinned. 'I told him I lived with my old and infirm mother and that she had a horrible temper.'

'Thanks a lot.' Norma laughed but sobered quickly. 'It's not the best way to start a relationship, you know, love. Not being honest, I mean. Not if it's really one that matters.'

'It matters, Mum.' Hannah caught the swing and stilled it. 'Had enough, button?'

'No—more!' Heidi shrieked happily. Hannah smiled and pushed her daughter away again.

'Do you think it matters as much to Adam?' Norma asked quietly.

'I hope so.' Hannah smiled shyly. 'He told me last night that he loved me and it wasn't the first time he's said that.' The colour rose in Hannah's cheeks. 'It *was* the first time I'd said it back, though.'

Norma spoke quietly after a short silence. 'It will only get harder to tell him the truth the longer you leave it.' Norma looked genuinely worried now.

'I know.' Hannah sighed heavily. 'Don't worry. I've got it all planned. We're crewing together on my day shift on Thursday. I'll make sure I tell him then.'

'If he loves you, it shouldn't make any difference,' Norma said confidently. She smiled at her granddaughter as Hannah finally lifted the child out of the swing. 'Nobody could fail to love our Heidi.'

'Maybe I should introduce them before I tell him, then.' Hannah smiled.

Norma chuckled. 'I wouldn't advise it. Let him get used to the idea first.'

Hannah was frowning as she cuddled Heidi. 'I hope it won't take too much getting used to.'

'Just make sure you tell him.'

'I will,' Hannah promised. 'It will be the very first thing I do on Thursday.'

CHAPTER FOUR

TALKING privately to Adam was the very last thing Hannah had the opportunity to do on Thursday morning.

In a carbon copy of the first time she had crewed with Adam, they had a priority-one call to a chest pain as soon as she arrived on duty. This time they entered the address to find their patient collapsed on the floor. A woman knelt beside him, sobbing hysterically.

'What's happened?' Adam asked.

Hannah crouched quickly and shook the man's shoulder. 'Hello, sir,' she said loudly. 'Can you hear me?'

'He said he had a funny feeling in his chest,' the woman told Adam. She pressed a hand to her mouth as she tried to control her sobs. 'And then he just collapsed.'

Hannah had checked the man's mouth for any obvious obstruction. Finding none, she tilted his head back to open the airway. She put her cheek near his face and rested her hand on his abdomen.

'Unresponsive and not breathing,' she informed Adam tersely.

'Oh, God, he's dead, isn't he?' The woman cried. 'Can't you *do* something?'

Adam flipped open his kit beside Hannah who reached for the bag mask unit. As she fitted the mask and squeezed the bag to give the patient two full breaths, Adam ripped the man's pyjama jacket open. A button flipped off and rolled across the floor towards the woman who backed away, watching in horror.

'Is this your husband?' Adam queried. The woman nodded. 'Does he have any history of cardiac problems?'

'No.'

Hannah had her hand on the man's neck. 'No pulse,' she reported. Without being told, Hannah positioned herself for single-person CPR, with her knees on either side of the man's head, leaning forward to compress his chest. She counted fifteen compressions and then sat back on her heels. She attached the portable oxygen cylinder to the bag mask unit, turned it on full and then positioned the mask to give another two ventilations.

Adam worked around her, positioning electrodes. He flicked the monitor on. 'Stop compressions,' he directed.

They both watched the interference from Hannah's movements clear from the screen and a trace appeared.

'VF,' Hannah murmured. She could recognise it quite easily now.

Adam nodded. 'Carry on CPR,' he ordered, reaching for a foil pack and ripping it open. He slapped the orange conduction pads on their patient's chest, one below the heart on the left side, the other near the electrode under the right collar-bone. Hannah was ventilating their patient again when Adam picked up the paddles. He positioned them on the orange pads.

'Are you clear?'

Hannah wriggled back so that her knees were no longer in contact with the patient. 'I'm clear,' she confirmed.

The man's body jerked as Adam delivered the shock. The static on the screen cleared to reveal no change.

'Continue CPR,' Adam directed. 'Charging again.'

Another shock of two hundred joules gave the same result.

'Charging to three-sixty,' Adam told Hannah. 'And then we'll intubate and call for back-up.'

Hannah nodded. She was doing chest compressions again and could feel a trickle of perspiration running down her back. Single-person CPR was hard work but she would have to keep it up while Adam made use of skills she didn't have. It was up to him to establish a secure airway, gain IV access and administer any drugs that might help.

'Stop compressions,' Adam ordered again. 'And stand clear.' He glanced up. 'Are you clear?'

'I'm clear.'

A groan came from the woman watching them in response to the patient's convulsive jerk. Adam glanced up again.

'We're doing everything we can,' he assured her. He reached for a pack in the bottom compartment of his kit. 'I'm going to put a tube down his throat now so we can breathe for him more effectively.'

Hannah was about to start compressions again but paused to touch Adam's arm.

'Adam, look,' she breathed, her eyes fastened on the monitor. The disturbances caused by the last shock had cleared to reveal a normal-looking trace.

Adam's hand went to the man's neck. 'Good pulse, too,' he said with satisfaction.

Their patient took his first spontaneous breath and Adam looked up to catch Hannah's gaze. She knew her excitement at their success must be written all over her face. Adam's smile told her he understood exactly how she felt.

The man's breathing became more regular and Hannah could stop assisting him with the bag mask. He moved slightly and groaned.

'Put a high-concentration oxygen mask on,' Adam directed. 'We'll establish IV access in case this doesn't last.'

Hannah took only a moment to fit the mask. Then she passed Adam an antiseptic wipe, the IV cannula he chose and a luer plug to fit on the end. She reached for a 5-ml ampoule of saline and a syringe to draw up the fluid to flush the line. For once she managed the task without fumbling or being slow with a single component. She handed the flush to Adam and was then ready with the sticky plastic cover and tape to hold the IV line in place.

Even filling in the paperwork was a breeze in the euphoria that came after the successful resuscitation. Their patient had regained consciousness by the time they had him on a stretcher, and he was able to help his stunned wife give Hannah all the relevant information she needed to record.

'He was only thirty-five,' she told Adam later as they completed the paperwork in the emergency department. 'And he's always been perfectly fit and healthy. He doesn't even smoke.'

'There's no sign of an infarct on the ECG either,' Adam mused. 'Could be a conduction defect that triggered the arrhythmia. We'll check later and see what the doctors can tell us.'

'Do you think he'll be OK?' Hannah queried anxiously. 'He's so young.'

Adam grinned. 'I'm glad you think so. I'm thirty-five as well, you know.'

Hannah returned the grin but she wasn't going to be distracted onto personal ground quite so easily. 'That's the first successful resuscitation I've had.'

'Congratulations.' Adam was still smiling. 'You've saved your first life.' The expression in Adam's dark eyes was one of shared joy. He took pleasure in her excitement and he was proud of her.

Hannah's smile was a little poignant a few minutes later

as she finished tidying the back of the ambulance. She zipped up the bag attached to the portable oxygen cylinder, having replaced the high-concentration, non-rebreather mask they had used. Then she climbed through to the front where she sat in her seat to wait for Adam. He was still inside the emergency department, checking in with the control room by phone.

'We've got a plane to meet at the airport,' Adam relayed as he joined her. 'A spinal transfer.'

'Slow transport?'

Adam nodded wearily and Hannah smiled. The very slow and careful pace they needed to drive when transferring an unstable spinal fracture was about the biggest contrast available to a high-priority call. They wouldn't be saving any more lives for a while this morning.

Hannah collected the signs which would slot onto the back doors of the ambulance and warn drivers of their slow speed and the need to pass the vehicle with care.

'I love this job,' she informed Adam as they headed towards the airport. 'You just never know what's coming next.'

'Life's full of surprises,' Adam concurred.

Hannah bit her bottom lip thoughtfully. She had a surprise for Adam and now seemed as good a time as any to broach the subject. Hannah swallowed nervously as she felt her pulse rate trip and then increase. She wished, desperately, that she had told him about her daughter weeks ago. It might have been an unpleasant surprise then but it was going to be far more of a shock now. And she had so much more to lose. Weeks ago it had been the stirrings of desire she had been reluctant to forgo. Now she was only too aware of the depth of her real attachment to Adam. Hannah struggled to summon the necessary courage. It wasn't going to get any easier if she postponed the inevitable yet again.

'Hey!' Adam reached out and touched Hannah's arm. He grinned as soon as he caught her eye. 'You saved a life today.'

'I helped,' Hannah corrected. Then a smile lit her own features. '*We* saved a life today.'

'Sure did.' Adam turned towards her again. 'We're an awesome team.'

'Sure are.' Hannah let herself bask, just for a second, in the warmth of Adam's gaze. It stirred an emotion far stronger than mere desire or even what she had previously considered love. She wanted this man to share any joy she experienced for the rest of her life.

Adam was watching the road again as they entered the Mount Victoria tunnel. 'Did you hear what happened to Eddie yesterday?'

'No.' Hannah grasped the new conversational direction as though it were some kind of lifeline. Just a tiny postponement, she assured herself. She would tell Adam before they reached the airport. 'What happened?'

'He broke his leg.'

'What?' Hannah was astonished. 'How did he do that?'

'He fell out of the back of an ambulance.' Adam guiltily wiped a smile off his face. 'Apparently he was so keen to get out when they answered a priority-one call that he missed his footing when he opened the back door and stepped out into space.'

'Oh, no! Poor Eddie.' Even Hannah found it difficult not to smile at the mental picture Adam's words evoked.

'Nasty fracture.' Adam looked quite serious now. 'Midshaft femur.'

'Who was he on with?'

'Gary. He called for backup and they put a Hare traction splint on Eddie and filled him up with morphine. He wasn't a happy lad. He's going to be off work for a couple of months at least.'

'What happened to the patient they were called to?'

'It wasn't anything major, fortunately. They ended up with three ambulances parked in their driveway and quite enjoyed the drama, by the sound of it.'

'Eddie must be upset.' Hannah smiled wryly. 'He'll miss the driving course and the next training sessions. And he's so determined to go places in this job.'

'He'll be going slowly for a while. I expect he'll be on crutches for weeks.'

'How's Michael doing?' Hannah had seen very little of some of her classmates since they had been absorbed into regular shift work.

'He had an argument with the paramedic—Jim Melton—he was working with last week. Michael was convinced he knew what was wrong with the patient and their opinions didn't exactly coincide.'

'Oh, no!' Hannah repeated. Maybe she wasn't doing too badly after all. She'd had no major disasters yet. 'What happened?' she asked curiously.

Adam finished telling Hannah about the inevitable blow to Michael's level of confidence in his own abilities as they reached the security gates that led onto the tarmac bordering one of the airport's runways. A guard waved them through and Adam pointed to a light aircraft taxiing towards them.

'Good timing,' he said approvingly. 'I was expecting to wait for at least half an hour.'

Hannah had been expecting a wait as well. She had planned to use the time to tell Adam what she had to tell him. Now the opportunity was gone and another was unlikely to present itself for quite some time. It would take over an hour to drive their patient at snail's pace to the specialist spinal unit in one of the city's outlying hospitals in the Hutt Valley.

More than two hours had passed by the time the job was completed because the medical team accompanying the patient had to be taken back to the airport along with the bulky equipment they had used. No sooner had the security guard finally let them out through the airport security gates than a new call came over their pagers.

Adam was the first to read the message. 'Priority two,' he announced. Then he groaned in disgust. 'It's a day-care centre.' He cast Hannah a long-suffering look. 'Brace yourself,' he warned. 'It'll probably be a rug rat.'

Hannah didn't acknowledge the comment. She gritted her teeth. If it got any harder than this, it would become totally impossible to tell Adam about Heidi. She scrolled her pager to get the address of the day-care centre as Adam activated the beacons. A priority-two call was still serious enough to warrant the use of lights and sirens.

'It's Rupert Bear's Pre-school!' she gasped a second later.

'Told you.' Adam sounded smug. 'Bound to be some ghastly child. Seeing as it's a day-care centre, it's probably also a serious injury.' His face set into grim lines as he turned on the siren and accelerated into the clear path that magically appeared in the traffic.

'Why did you say that?' Hannah was trying to keep a lid on the fingers of fear she could feel clutching at her. Heidi went to Rupert Bear's Pre-school. She was probably there right now as the morning session had finished only minutes ago.

'Safety standards are bloody non-existent at some of these places,' Adam said disgustedly. 'Personally, I wouldn't leave a dog there.'

Hannah curled her hands into tight fists and pressed her lips together hard. She should never have taken this job. She should be at home, caring for her precious child as she had done for the first two years of her life. God, what if it *was* Heidi who had been injured? Hannah closed her eyes for a second to speak firmly to herself and gain control.

It wasn't true about safety standards. That had been an issue Hannah and Norma had been particularly careful to check on when they'd made their extensive tour of the city's child-care facilities. Rupert Bear's had been as good as any. The staff were all practically surrogate mothers and Hannah had had no hesitation in trusting them with the welfare of her child.

She only heard Adam when he raised his voice to a shout.

'I need a map reference, Hannah. Come on, wake up!' Adam leaned on the air horn as a car failed to move aside ahead of them. The startled driver swerved and Adam put his foot down and surged past up the steep hill.

'I don't need a map.' Hannah was astonished at how calm she sounded. 'I know where the centre is. Turn left at the next set of lights.'

'Thank you.' Adam sounded sarcastic and Hannah flinched. He was in a bad mood and it could well become a lot worse. Even the thought of being around children seemed to be enough to upset the man, but right now Hannah couldn't even begin to consider the implications of Adam discovering her connection to Rupert Bear's Pre-school. Her anxiety was centred entirely on her tiny, defenceless daughter.

Rupert Bear's manager, Cheryl, was waiting for them in the car park. 'Thank goodness you're here!' she exclaimed. 'Come this way—it's one of the children.'

Hannah scrambled out and rounded the front of the ambulance. 'Who is it?' she queried sharply.

'What's happened exactly?' Adam asked at the same moment. He was leaning out of his window.

Cheryl looked from Hannah to Adam, wondering which question to answer. She did a double-take and returned her gaze to Hannah.

'Good heavens, it's you, Hannah!' Cheryl's smile was fleeting. 'I almost didn't recognise you in your uniform.'

'What's the problem, here, madam?' Adam broke in abruptly.

Cheryl's attention snapped back. 'It's Shane. He's three years old.'

Hannah breathed an audible sigh of relief. It wasn't Heidi.

'He dived off the couch and landed on his hands. I think he may have broken his collar-bone.' Cheryl shook her head worriedly. 'Normally, we'd take a child to the hospital or a doctor ourselves, but the poor wee chap's in such a lot of pain. I knew we needed some help.'

Cheryl began walking towards the door as she spoke. Hannah was right beside her. They were almost inside the building by the time Adam caught up. His pace seemed leisurely and Hannah was annoyed by his apparent lack of urgency. At least he was carrying his kit.

Shane lay in the arms of another centre staff member. Megan looked nearly as pale as the child she held. She was stroking his hair and trying to soothe the small boy who sounded exhausted but was still managing some heart-rending whimpers.

Adam crouched beside them. 'Hi, there, Shane,' he said cheerfully. 'My name's Adam.'

Shane turned to bury his face in Megan's shoulder. The movement made him cry out with renewed energy. Adam seemed happy to give up trying to establish a rapport with the child.

'Use your shears, Hannah,' he directed. 'Let's get this jersey off so we can see what we're dealing with.'

Hannah took the shears from her belt. She was loath to cut the jersey, knowing how proud Shane was of the Teletubby design his mother had painstakingly knitted into the garment. Her hesitation made her aware of the anxious adult faces watching from the dining-room window. Several mothers had arrived to collect their children but they were clearly waiting for the drama to be over. The staff were keeping the children clear of the scene by providing their lunch. Hannah was relieved not to see Norma amongst the small audience. Maybe she had collected Heidi early and was already home.

Hannah's few seconds' hesitation made Adam clear his throat impatiently. She turned hurriedly to her task, clipping the sleeve of the jersey clear and then also cutting away the long-sleeved T-shirt Shane was wearing. Adam quickly examined the child.

'He's definitely broken his collar-bone,' he stated, 'but I'm more concerned about this elbow.'

Hannah could see the odd lump protruding from Shane's arm. Was the elbow broken or dislocated? Adam tried to feel for a radial pulse but Shane shrieked in fear and tried to pull his arm away.

'We'll have to get an IV in,' Adam said calmly, 'and give him some pain relief.' He turned to Cheryl who was watching with obvious concern. 'Can you help hold him, please? We need to turn him so we can reach his uninjured side. Hannah, you'll have to get a good grip on his arm so I can get a line in his hand.' Adam flipped open his kit. 'He's not going to like this but he'll be much happier when we can get a bit of morphine on board.'

Not liking the procedure was an understatement. Hannah felt quite shaky herself by the time it was over. Holding a child to comfort it was one thing. Holding it so that more pain could be inflicted was entirely different and difficult to do, even knowing the benefit to be gained. To his credit, Adam completed the tricky task in minimum time. Within five minutes the line was in and taped firmly into place, narcotic pain relief had been administered and the injured arm was splinted against Shane's body with triangular bandages. Shane had stopped crying. He lay drowsily in Cheryl's arms now.

'I want Mummy,' he said sleepily.

'I know, darling.' Cheryl gave him a kiss. 'Mummy's going to be waiting for us at the hospital.' She looked up at Adam. 'Shall I carry him out for you?'

Adam nodded. 'Are you going to come with us?'

'Of course. I wouldn't leave him with strangers. He doesn't know Hannah that well and she looks different in uniform anyway.'

'Oh?' Adam was busy closing the lid of his kit. Hannah hastily distracted Cheryl.

'Come with me,' she invited the older woman. 'I'll get a bed ready for you to sit on and you can keep holding Shane.'

Some children had finished their lunch and were now outside, playing. A couple of mothers were leading their offspring towards the car park. Hannah settled Cheryl on the stretcher and then jumped down to fold the back step of the ambulance away. Suddenly one of the children leaving the centre broke away from her companion.

'Mumma!' The shriek was a joyous crow. Heidi's face was wreathed in a huge grin as she ran towards Hannah. As Hannah stooped to catch her daughter, Norma arrived by her side.

Adam arrived at her other side.

'Good heavens,' Norma exclaimed. 'I didn't realise it was *you* looking after Shane, love.'

'I thought you'd gone home already,' Hannah countered in despair. She let Heidi go. 'I've got to go now,' she explained.

Heidi's blue eyes widened. 'Me, too, Mumma.'

'No. Sorry, darling. You're going home with Nanna.'

Adam was staring at Heidi. He looked as though he had happened across a rare and particularly obnoxious form of wildlife. Norma and Hannah exchanged meaningful glances.

'Mum, this is Adam Lewis,' Hannah said unhappily.

'Hello, Adam.' Norma's smile was friendly. 'I've heard about you.'

'This is my mother, Adam,' Hannah continued doggedly. 'Norma Duncan.'

'Hello, Norma.' Adam's expression was still stunned. 'I've heard about you as well. How's the arthritis today?'

'Uh…' Norma looked helplessly at Hannah.

'I'll see you later, Mum.' Hannah filled the very awkward silence rapidly. 'We've got to get Shane off to Emergency now.'

Norma looked relieved. She picked Heidi up as Adam nodded curtly and stepped past. Heidi was grinning again. She waved both hands vigorously.

'Bye, Mumma.'

'Bye, darling.' Hannah pulled the back doors shut. She sat down on the second stretcher with a lurch as Adam pulled away abruptly. A glance towards the front of the ambulance gave her a picture of Adam's face in the rear-view mirror. She had never seen him look quite so grim. With a sigh, Hannah picked up the patient report form book.

'Tell me again what happened exactly, Cheryl.'

Hannah was left in charge of the hand-over in Emergency.

'This is Shane Dawson,' she informed the triage nurse. 'He's three years old. He dived off a couch about fifty centimetres high and landed on his right hand. He's fractured his collar-bone and we're querying a fracture/dislocation of his right elbow.'

The nurse tilted her head to smile at Shane. 'Hello, sweetheart. Your mummy's in the waiting room. She'll be here in just a minute.'

'He's had 1.5 mg of morphine to good effect,' Hannah added. She handed the top copy of the patient report form to the nurse.

'Cubicle 4, thanks,' the nurse directed. 'I'll send someone to get his mother.'

'I'll go,' Hannah offered. 'I know what she looks like.'

Natasha Dawson was pacing the waiting-room area. Hannah smiled reassuringly. 'Shane's OK, Natasha. He's had some pain relief and is quite sleepy. He's going to be very pleased to see you.' Hannah led the way into the emergency department.

'I knew something like this would happen.' Natasha Dawson sighed. 'I was about to clinch the deal on this house sale when I got the phone call. My clients weren't too pleased when I had to rush off. If I lose the sale my boss will be furious, but what could I do? Shane's far more important.'

'Of course he is. I'd do exactly the same,' Hannah agreed.

'I don't really *have* to work,' Natasha confessed as they passed the sluice room in the corridor. 'Not financially, I mean. But I love my job. I'd be miserable stuck at home all day, and what sort of mother would I be then?'

Hannah nodded. She recognised the pattern of guilt only too well.

'And Shane loves day care. He's an only child so it gives him the opportunity to be with other children.'

Hannah touched the young mother's arm. 'This accident could have happened at home just as easily. You don't have to justify your reasons for using day care. Nobody's going to think you're a bad mother.'

Except maybe Adam Lewis.

Hannah expected the subject to be raised as soon as they were confined in the privacy of the ambulance again but Adam said nothing. They drove in silence until a pager message came through. It was a low-priority case—a transfer on a doctor's recommendation from one of the larger local rest homes. Hannah reached for the street map.

'I know where it is,' Adam snapped. 'I've been there a hundred times.'

'I haven't,' Hannah responded quietly. 'I'd like to know where we're going. It's good practice for me.'

Adam made no response. Hannah watched his profile for several seconds. The small bump on the bridge of his nose was pale, the jaw muscles bunched. Clearly Adam was too upset to want to talk right now and Hannah knew she would have to wait until he was ready. With an inaudible sigh she turned to the street index.

Adam still wasn't ready to talk on the way to their next call. When they finally reached headquarters, having made two further calls, Adam disappeared into the storeroom. Hannah knew she should help restock the ambulance but was reluctant to follow Adam into the small room, with other staff members likely to interrupt at any moment. This was no place to have a private conversation. The

main oxygen cylinder needed changing in any case and
Hannah gratefully attended to the task. By the time she
had finished they received their final call for the shift.

Having delivered their patient, they left the hospital
nearly an hour later, detouring away from the route back
to headquarters in order to refuel. By the time they left
the service station Hannah had convinced herself that
Adam had no intention of talking to her during working
hours. He then startled her by pulling off the road near
the entrance to the zoological gardens and switching off
the engine. He turned the radio transmitter off, cutting the
background noise of messages to and from other crews
and the control room. They sat in complete silence for
nearly a minute. Hannah waited. This was it.

It was Adam who broke the tense silence,

'So.' The tone was heavy. 'That was your mother, was
it?'

'Yes.' Hannah kept her head bent, her eyes focused on
her hands.

'The woman who is too crippled with arthritis to live
by herself.'

Hannah said nothing. Norma was only fifty-nine and
the picture of health in anyone's book.

'The woman who hates strangers coming to her house
and is inclined to be unpleasantly ill-tempered?'

Hannah cringed. How many of her fabrications was he
going to throw back at her? OK, she hadn't been entirely
honest but there had been good reasons for that. Hannah
felt the stirrings of anger. Adam had spent all afternoon
planning this attack. If he wanted to make this a nasty
experience then she wasn't going to go down without a
fight. If nothing else, Hannah intended to preserve her
dignity.

'Actually, she's a very nice person,' Hannah said

firmly. 'I moved back in with her just before Heidi was born. It was the best thing I could have done.'

'Heidi?' Adam was naming the undesirable form of wildlife.

'My daughter.' God, it felt good to get the word past her lips in the company of Adam Lewis. Hannah felt a wash of pride. Nobody was ever going to make her reluctant to admit to her status as a mother again. 'She's two and a half,' Hannah continued, 'and she's a very special little person.' A glance at Adam's face made Hannah falter momentarily in her new resolution. 'I've been trying to find a way to tell you about her.'

Adam's snort was contemptuous. 'How hard can it be, Hannah? You've had weeks—no, *months*—to tell me. You could have thrown it into a conversation at any time. Look at the way Christine never stopped talking about *her* bloody kids.'

'Exactly!' Hannah met Adam's glare. 'And you were on her back about being a working mother for the whole induction period. I didn't need that kind of extra pressure.'

'I was *not* on her back.' Adam's tone was a warning.

Hannah ignored the warning. 'You were so,' she contradicted. 'You made it quite clear that you thought she wouldn't be able to do the job properly. And you didn't let her get away with even a slight hiccup. She failed that course the moment she had that phone call about her son's accident.'

'I didn't fail her,' Adam said angrily. 'She chose not to continue.'

'And who persuaded her, I wonder?' Hannah shot back. 'Are you trying to deny that you're prejudiced against working mothers?'

'*You* didn't exactly fail, did you?'

'You didn't know I was a mother.'

Adam looked away. He drummed his fingers on the steering-wheel. 'You could have told me after you got the damned job.'

'Oh, sure,' Hannah said scathingly. 'When—after we went to that call and you said you had no intention of ever finding out what it was like, juggling motherhood and a career?'

Adam continued to stare ahead. His fingers kept up the irritating tattoo on the wheel.

'Or after every time you called children rug rats, or ankle-biters or snotty-nosed brats?' Hannah's voice rose. 'Or maybe I could have slipped it in after you said you wouldn't even leave a dog in a day-care centre.' Her throat was starting to constrict. 'You hate kids. Everybody knows that.'

Adam's fingers stilled. The silence grew but Adam still wouldn't look at Hannah. When he spoke, his voice was as empty as his face.

'I thought we had something special going here.'

The constriction in Hannah's throat was becoming painful. 'I thought so, too.'

'No, you didn't.' Adam's gaze met Hannah's. The depth of disappointment she could see hit her as a solid force. 'I meant *really* special. Something with a future.'

'My child is a very big part of my future, Adam,' Hannah said softly. 'She's a part of me.'

'My future doesn't include children. Mine…or anyone else's. I think you knew that already, didn't you, Hannah? You knew this would be over as soon as I found out about your daughter. That's why you didn't tell me.'

Hannah couldn't swallow now. It would be nice to cry—it might begin to melt the painful lump threatening to choke her. But tears weren't on the agenda. Not yet.

'I guess that's it, then. There's no future for us.'

'I guess not,' Adam replied. 'I'm sorry, Hannah.'

'I'm sorry, too.' Hannah watched as Adam moved in slow motion, starting the vehicle and pulling away from the side of the road. 'I knew this wasn't a good idea.'

'What, being dishonest?' Adam queried coldly.

'No.' Hannah's voice was tight. 'Having a personal relationship with a colleague. It's not going to be easy working together now, is it?'

'We'll cope,' Adam responded coolly. 'At least, I will.' He gave Hannah only the briefest glance. 'It happened,' he said evenly. 'And it's over. I have no intention of letting it interfere with the rest of my life. Neither should you.'

Hannah said nothing. She had no words available.

'Nobody knows about us.' Adam waited for the automatic doors of the garage to open. 'I don't really think it will be too much of a problem.' He nodded to himself as he jumped out of the vehicle and slammed the door shut behind him.

He'd coped with worse than this. Shutting Hannah out of his life would be no problem at all.

CHAPTER FIVE

IT WAS a huge problem.

Adam had seriously underestimated the difficulty he was going to experience cutting Hannah from his personal life. Initially, the anger was a considerable bonus. Adam fed it whenever possible. The woman had led him on, encouraged his physical attraction until the point that he'd fallen in love with her. He'd even *told* her he loved her, for God's sake. He'd only ever said that to one other woman in his life. And she still hadn't had the decency to tell him that there was no way they could ever have any kind of future together. Even though she knew, as well as anybody else, how Adam felt about children.

Adam sent Hannah the blackest look he could dredge up but she remained apparently unaware of his presence in the garage. The heavy rain on the corrugated-iron roofing covered any sound he was making while checking his vehicle. Now he had his paramedic kit open on the front seat, scrutinising the contents. Hannah was preoccupied with changing the large oxygen cylinder on the ambulance parked alongside Unit 241. Undoing the straps that held the tank behind the front passenger seat, she eased the cylinder free and carried it to the supply area where she selected a full replacement. Hannah's slight figure and average height made the burden look too large to be comfortably managed. The urge to offer assistance was automatic and Adam suppressed it with a fierce flash of irritation.

Tom Bagshaw arrived for the start of his day shift as

Hannah's partner. He was yawning, which wasn't unusual these days. His first child had arrived a couple of months earlier and Tom was proud of the fact that he was losing as much sleep as his wife. Adam scowled at Tom.

'You're bright-eyed and bushy-tailed again, I see.'

Tom grinned. 'It's worth it, mate.'

Hannah's head had swung around sharply at the sound of Adam's voice but apparently it was only Tom that was visible to her. 'Hi, Tom. How are you?'

'Stuffed,' Tom told her cheerfully. 'I was up four times last night. Want a hand with the oxygen?'

'No, I can manage.' Hannah was screwing the regulator onto the top of the cylinder.

'I'll get us a toaster, then.'

Hannah smiled. She had already checked out and installed the life pack. 'Been there, done that,' she told Tom.

'Excellent! We're ready to roll, then?'

Hannah wiped her hands on a cloth. 'The sooner the better,' she agreed lightly. 'We just need to do the mechanical check.'

Adam slammed the lid of his kit down and snapped the catch into place. Hannah probably thought she was being subtle but he was aware of every nuance. The only reason she was so keen to get out on the road was to get away from his presence. The last shift had been tense to say the least after the argument on Thursday. Fortunately they hadn't crewed together the next day. On the two night shifts, Hannah and Adam had both made use of the bedrooms above the garage after midnight, emerging only when they had calls. As they still weren't crewing the same vehicle, their times out hadn't coincided at all. Adam had hoped that their four days off might have been enough time for the tension to dissipate but now he real-

ised, with increasing dismay, that it seemed to have
grown.

Why on earth had he been so keen to ensure that
Hannah was assigned to Blue shift? Why, for that matter,
had he let her pass the induction course so successfully?
Adam stowed his kit in the back of the ambulance and
pulled open an overhead locker to check the supply of
oxygen masks. He could still see Hannah. She was standing in front of the neighbouring vehicle, giving Tom a
thumbs-up sign as he turned on the indicators and headlights. The siren was given a quick blast and then the
beacons were checked. The bright flash of the alternating
headlights caught Hannah, and the silver colour of her hair
shone as brightly as a Christmas-tree decoration. Adam
slammed the locker shut.

Of course he couldn't have failed Hannah. He would
still have been happy to have her working on Blue shift.
What he could—no, would have done, however, was to
ensure that any indulgence of his attraction to her remained firmly out of bounds. That way, he could have
enjoyed her company, appreciated her skill and looked
forward to a long and happy professional relationship. The
only bright spot in the bleak situation at present was that
none of their colleagues knew what a fool he had made
of himself.

Adam's partner, Matt, arrived at work. 'Weren't you
supposed to be third call today?' he asked Adam.

'I got swapped,' Adam responded. He hoped Hannah
was listening. 'With Tom.' Would Hannah think it was
him rather than the station manager who had initiated the
change?

'Lucky me.' Tom grinned.

'I know why he got swapped,' Matt told Tom. 'It's the
PR job you've got lined up at 9 a.m.'

'What's that?' Hannah queried.

'The whole junior department at Naseby Street school.' Matt clipped his pager onto his belt. 'Can you imagine what it would do for public relations if Adam got sent to deal with that many kids?'

Tom laughed. Hannah didn't even smile. Neither did Adam. He turned and stalked off in the direction of the storeroom.

'Someone got out of bed on the wrong side this morning,' he heard Matt comment.

'It's the thought of all those vertically challenged people.' Tom was still highly amused. 'It's the stuff of nightmares for our Adam.'

Adam shoved the storeroom door open and let it swing shut behind him. Why had he always been so happy to foster the rumour that he hated children? Maybe, if Hannah knew the truth, she would realise the extent of the damage she'd done. She would know that she had absolutely no justification in being as angry as he now was.

Adam pulled a couple of nebuliser masks from their carton and scanned the shelves for the other items he needed to restock. Nobody here knew the truth. That part of his life had been over the day he had moved to this city and this job. It had been years ago. Buried well enough for Adam to be able to cope easily with his life. He had found the way to move on and he wasn't about to start going backwards. Adam had no intention of telling anybody about the past. Including Hannah Duncan.

Hannah's and Tom's first call for the day was a transfer. An elderly patient was going to a nursing home to complete her recuperation following surgery. They collected the woman well before 8 a.m. but it was a forty-five-minute drive out to the Upper Hutt suburb of Silverstream. By the time they had delivered their patient and turned back towards the city it was 8.30 a.m. The torrential rain had ceased and the strong winds were now sending the clouds scudding towards Australia. The sun was doing its best to make an impression during the brief gaps in the cloud cover.

'We're not going to make it to that school on time,' Hannah observed.

'No.' Tom looked thoughtful as he picked up the microphone. 'Unit 225 to Control.'

'Go ahead, 225.'

'We're heading back into town,' Tom reported. 'We won't make Naseby Street before 9.30 a.m.' He winked at Hannah. 'Maybe you should send Unit 241.'

Hannah's eyes widened. If Adam was in his vehicle he would hear the transmission. She could imagine his reaction to the teasing. Hannah couldn't help a small smile escaping. Adam was already less than happy, but why shouldn't he suffer just as much as she was? The past week had been miserable for Hannah.

OK, she'd been wrong not to tell Adam about Heidi, but why should her daughter's existence be such a catastrophe? If Adam felt the same way about Hannah as she felt about him then he would be prepared to at least try and accept other parts of her life. If their positions were reversed and Adam had a child, it certainly wouldn't have put Hannah off continuing their relationship.

The control room took a minute to respond to Tom's suggestion. 'Negative, 225. Naseby Street is happy to wait.'

Tom shook his head as he replaced the microphone. 'Adam's off the hook.'

'Why *does* he hate children so much?' Hannah asked curiously.

'I've got no idea.' Tom shrugged. 'I can't understand it myself.' He grinned at Hannah. 'Did I tell you that Harry's started smiling now?'

'You did.'

'I think he might be getting a tooth.'

'It's a bit early at eight weeks,' Hannah said. 'Heidi didn't get her first tooth until she was eight months.'

'Some babies are born with their first tooth through,' Tom stated. 'I read it in one of our baby books.'

Hannah just nodded. Tom was revelling in his new role as a father. His surprise, last week, when Hannah had told him she was a mother had quickly given way to making the most of the opportunities to discuss babies with another parent. Right now Hannah was more interested in another topic of conversation.

'How long have you known Adam?' she queried.

'Four years,' Tom answered. 'He was already here when I got a job. That was just after Jane and I got married,' he continued. 'Do you know, it took us nearly three years to get pregnant?' Hannah did already know. She hoped that Tom would be as keen to talk about someone else as he was about himself. 'Has Adam ever been married?'

Tom looked surprised. 'What makes you ask?' Then he smiled slowly. 'Are you interested?'

Hannah laughed—lightly, she hoped. 'Not at all. I'm just curious. He never says much about his past.'

'Unlike me, you mean.' Tom smiled. He accelerated to pass a container truck heading for the wharves and remained silent until he had completed the manoeuvre. 'There *was* a rumour that Adam had been married once but you know what this place is like for gossip and, as you say, Adam doesn't talk about himself much.'

'How long has he worked here?'

'About five years, I think, but he's been in the service for a lot longer than that. He did all his training in Australia and he was already a paramedic when he came to New Zealand.'

Hannah hesitated only briefly. 'I guess he's had a relationship or two since he's been here.'

'He's never been short of a partner on social occasions,' Tom said with a nod. 'But I don't think I've ever seen him with the same woman more than once.' His glance was amused this time. 'Are you sure you're not interested?'

'I like working with him,' Hannah admitted. 'And I enjoyed my induction course. He's a brilliant teacher. I suppose I'm just surprised that he's not married.'

She should have asked him herself while they had still been talking to each other. There had been enough opportunities but Hannah's instincts had warned her to concentrate on and enjoy the present. If Adam had been forthcoming about his personal history, she would have been obliged to follow suit. It had been much easier to consider it fair enough that they'd both had things they hadn't been ready to share. Adam's house hadn't provided any obvious clues to his past. Hannah had to admit she'd looked for them. It wasn't that the clean lines of the modern dwelling weren't softened by personal touches. There were hundreds of books and lots of interesting works of art but she hadn't seen a single photograph on display.

'Shift work can put a lot of stress on marriages,' Tom commented, breaking the short silence. 'Especially when you've got a young family. Maybe he just wants to avoid the hassle.' Tom grinned. 'Not everybody can take the

pressure of non-stop howling, night-time feeds and end-
less nappy changes.'

'Unlike you.' Hannah smiled.

'That's right,' Tom said proudly. Then he sighed. 'How
old was your daughter when she started sleeping through
the night?'

'About six months.' Hannah settled back, resigned to
talking babies for the rest of the journey. At least it would
provide a welcome distraction to thinking about Adam,
which only fuelled the anger she had lived with for the
last week. 'Of course, when Heidi started teething it was
back to square one.'

The Naseby Street school job was a great success.

'Hannah's a regular Mother Goose,' Tom informed
their colleagues later that day. 'She had a hundred and
fifty kids eating out of her hand.'

'Maybe you should have been a teacher,' Matt told
Hannah.

'She still could be.' This came from Adam who had
appeared to have his full attention focused on the newspaper in front of him. 'She's bound to get sick of having
to work with you lot.'

Hannah glared at the back of Adam's head as she
reached for the coffee tin. 'I've chosen my career, thanks.'

'Yeah, don't give her any ideas, Adam,' Tom admonished. 'We like having Hannah around.'

'Plenty of kids to deal with in this job, anyway,' Matt
added. 'Isn't that right, Adam?'

Adam grunted noncommittally and turned the page of
the newspaper.

Tom sat down at the long table in the headquarter's
staffroom. 'Nearly time to go home,' he said with satis-

faction. 'What exciting plans have you got lined up for this evening, Hannah?'

'Just the usual,' Hannah responded. 'I'll give Heidi her bath and read her a story. Then I'll probably do something really boring like washing my hair.'

Adam turned another page. Why couldn't he find an article that was at least remotely interesting? He had to find some way of quashing the mental image of Hannah cuddled up on a couch with a freshly powdered, tousled-haired small girl in the crook of her arm. He could almost hear her lilting, soft voice and laughter bringing a story to life.

He pushed back his chair abruptly. 'I'm going to wash the truck,' he informed his partner.

The activity didn't help as much as he'd hoped. Adam watched the curls of steam and soap bubbles as he filled the stainless-steel bucket. Now he couldn't help imagining Hannah washing her hair. Or, worse, combing it out while it dried, ripples of silver cloaking her back. He knew what it felt like to gather the soft weight back in his hands. He could almost feel the tickle of it cascading onto his bare skin. Adam swore under his breath as the bucket over-flowed.

Wrenching the tap off, Adam reached for the soft broom. He'd be able to get away from this place shortly, and maybe away from Hannah's physical presence he could control his thoughts more easily. He'd pick up one of his favourite Indian take-away meals on the way home and kick back with a glass of red wine and some music. Or, even better, a good book. Adam had always had the pleasure of being able to escape easily into fiction. To forget his own worries and focus on the plight and even-tual resolution of the problems faced by the fictional char-acters.

Only this time it didn't work. For some reason, one of his preferred authors was failing to capture him. The characters were cardboard and their conflicts lacked enough reality to distract him from real life. The hero had no real idea what it was like to fall in love. The author had probably never really fallen for anybody. Not the way Adam had fallen for Hannah at any rate.

Then again, maybe he had it all wrong. Maybe he wasn't in love with Hannah at all. He'd been in love with Linda, hadn't he? In love enough to marry her. He'd never been obsessed with her like this, however. She hadn't crept into every waking thought. He'd never had that adrenaline rush that went with the anticipation of seeing Hannah. He'd never had to actually exert physical control to keep from constantly touching her. He'd never even thought to question the quality of the relationship he'd had with Linda. Until now.

The book Adam had been reading seemed to close of its own accord. He exchanged it for the glass of wine on the table without conscious thought. The signpost to memory lane had passed already and it had forgotten to flash its customary warning signal.

Quiet, brave Linda. Brave because so many things had frightened her and yet she had found the courage to face them. Like the difficult pregnancy and the interminable and badly managed labour she'd gone through to have their child. She hadn't even complained of feeling more than a little unwell after the birth. She'd accepted the overworked registrar's verdict of flu and had persuaded Adam not to make a fuss on her behalf. Linda had remained stoical for another two days until it had become alarmingly obvious that it had been no virus causing her illness. It had been too late by then to deal effectively with the rampant post-partum infection. Linda had died when the daughter she had named Madison had been four days old.

Adam drained his glass and refilled it. There was no chance of changing direction now. He might as well follow the familiar, painful journey. It happened far more rarely these days. Perhaps, this time, it wouldn't be so bad.

There had been no one to help Adam during that dark time. No family help had been forthcoming from Adam's side and Linda's parents had blamed him and the baby for their daughter's death. The case had made the newspapers, hailed as another example of staff shortages and unacceptable pressures on staff leading to a diagnosis being wrongly made and a young life needlessly lost. The mediafest had continued as Linda's family had tried to sue the hospital but Adam had wanted no part of the debacle. He'd focused quietly on attending to the needs of his newborn child, channelling his grief into something he'd seen as the only light at the end of a very dark tunnel.

Adam had postponed taking up his newly won qualifications as a paramedic, taking a year's leave from work to care for his baby. Maddy had quickly changed from being a distraction from his grief to the centre of Adam's universe. The dark hair she'd had at birth had fallen out and gradually been replaced by silky blonde curls. The huge brown eyes and ready smile had melted everyone's hearts. Not many children had been so instantly appealing. Why, in God's name, did Hannah's daughter have to look so similar?

Or did she? Adam pushed his glass away and rose to his feet, drawn to do something he hadn't done for a very long time. Tucked into one of the bookshelves was a small, flat box. Standing on its end, it looked just like another book. Inside were the few precious reminders that

Adam had not been able to part with, however painful they were to touch. He hadn't even looked at them for nearly five years. Ever since he'd moved to a new country. A new life.

A hospital identification bracelet lay on top, along with a tiny, slightly yellowed pair of bootees and two wedding rings. The bottom of the box was lined with certificates from the registry of births, deaths and marriages. In between was an envelope containing photographs. At least fifty of them. One was of Adam and Linda on their wedding day. The rest were of Maddy.

Adam pulled the bottom photograph from the pile. Maddy had been exactly two and a half that day. Heidi's age. They weren't nearly as similar as Adam had feared. Maddy's eyes had been brown, not blue like Heidi's. Heidi's hair was thicker and a completely different shade. She would probably end up a silvery, ash blonde like her mother. Maddy's curls had been so fine they had hung in tiny corn-coloured ringlets. Maddy hadn't taken after her mother at all. Definitely not quiet and totally unafraid of anything. Did Heidi Duncan throw herself at life with the sheer zest Maddy had displayed? Adam hoped she didn't.

The image of the photograph blurred and Adam felt a familiar pain send its tentacles around his heart. This photograph had been the last one taken of his daughter. The day before she'd died. The regrets were still there. The 'if onlys' still ready to pounce.

If only Adam hadn't decided to go back to work, needing the challenge of more than simply parenthood, feeling like he'd done well devoting a full year to the nurture of his baby. If only he'd been able to afford a full-time nanny instead of having to compromise by using day care a few times a week. If only he hadn't been on duty the day of the accident. If only it could have been someone else who'd gone to that call to find the tiny girl with the head injury caused by falling from the tree. An injury that would never have happened if appropriate safety standards had been in place. An injury that had been too severe to allow Maddy to even regain consciousness.

The box slotted back into the bookshelf. The memories also slotted back into their long-established storage compartment. Adam accomplished the tidy-up with more ease than he had ever previously managed. He might even get through the night without a recurrence of the nightmare. He'd been right to bury things for so long. He'd also been right in his resolve to never allow himself to be drawn to another child. He wasn't even going to like children, let alone love one. There was no way he would ever let himself risk that kind of self-destruction again. He could close them out of his heart. He'd done it for more than five years. Ever since he'd crawled out of the mindless grief which had consumed him after Maddy's death.

Adam had closed women out for the same reason. No risk, no pain. It had been a successful strategy up till now. An occasional relationship, a bit of sex—nothing heavy. Nothing that the ending of which might form a void that couldn't be easily filled.

Why the hell was it proving so difficult to employ the same strategy with Hannah?

CHAPTER SIX

THIS wasn't going to be easy.

Hannah stared at the computer printout on the wall of the duty room. There was no mistake. She was crewing with Adam for the night and she would simply have to cope. But it wasn't going to be easy. It had been difficult enough on the two day shifts this week when Hannah had crewed with Tom and then Matt, only seeing Adam intermittently. Tonight she would be shut into the same vehicle, sitting only inches away, with the distraction of caring for patients confined to the return leg of each journey.

Adam clearly felt the same way. He didn't smile when he greeted Hannah and he took his kit into the storeroom to check while Hannah went over the supplies carried on board the ambulance. They both took their time. Hannah counted the lancets and testing strips for the blood-glucose kit. She checked all the expiry dates on the salbutamol ampoules and rearranged the overhead cupboard that contained IV fluids and giving sets, gloves and vomit containers.

Waiting until Adam left the storeroom, Hannah went to collect more of the last items. It was Sunday night and there had been an interprovincial rugby match that day which Wellington had won. There was bound to be at least one celebrating fan who had seriously overindulged. Probably more than one. Running short of the small plastic buckets was definitely a situation best avoided.

Unit 241 was on the road by 6.30 p.m. The job was a priority three, designating a response time of within thirty minutes. The patient wasn't believed to be in a life-threatening condition. The location was a rural maternity hospital twenty minutes' drive from the city. The patient was a newborn in an incubator who needed to be transferred to the neonatal ICU.

'Looks like it might rain,' Adam commented after several minutes silence.

'It *has* been colder today,' Hannah responded politely.

'We always get a lot of rain in September.'

'Do we?'

'Mmm.'

Hannah glanced sideways at Adam who kept his gaze firmly on the road ahead. Was this what their relationship had been reduced to? A polite conversation about the *weather*? It was probably preferable to a loaded silence, but only marginally. Hannah's quick glance was still enough to register the shadows under Adam's eyes and the accentuation of the nearby lines. Up until now Hannah had been pleased at the thought that he was suffering as much as she was. It was rather annoying to now feel a sudden surge of concern for the man. Hannah reached for the paperwork in the dashboard cubbyhole and filled in the date and crew details.

'What do we know about this patient?' Hannah queried. It had been Adam who had answered the control room link phone in the duty room.

'Born at thirty six weeks' gestation about two hours ago. He's not breathing quite well enough for the doctor to feel happy.'

Hannah wrote in the address of the maternity hospital and put 'Patient Transfer' in the type-of-incident space. At least the baby would be relatively quiet, shut inside an incubator. That shouldn't aggravate Adam too much.

'Is there a medical escort?'

'I think so.'

'Do we have a name?' Hannah eyed the patient details gaps.

'Just put Baby Mulligan.'

'Mulligan?'

Adam finally looked directly at Hannah. 'That's his surname.' He sounded surprised. 'What's wrong with that?'

'Nothing.' Hannah bit her lip. She knew she hadn't echoed the surname with any obvious dismay. How had Adam picked up on her reaction so easily? When he glanced at her for a second time, with a slight frown creasing his dark brows, Hannah gave a somewhat resigned sigh. At least it might be a way of ending discussions about the weather.

'It would have been my name,' she said quietly, 'if I had got married.' She paused only fractionally. 'To Heidi's father.'

'Why didn't you?' Adam's tone was clipped.

'He died,' Hannah responded simply. 'A few days after we discovered I was pregnant.'

Adam was silent for a long minute. 'So you *were* planning to get married, then?'

'Of course. We had been engaged for two years. We met in London but I wanted to wait until we came back to New Zealand before we got married. We loved each other very much,' Hannah continued softly. 'And we were very excited about the baby.'

The silence was even longer this time. Was Adam comparing himself to Ben—a man Hannah had loved and who had *wanted* children?

'So what happened?' Adam queried abruptly.

'He drowned,' Hannah said tersely. Then she sighed again, more heavily this time. 'No, that's not true, really. He had a congenital heart problem which had never been picked up. His heart just stopped and he died instantly. He just happened to be swimming at the time.'

They were almost at their destination before Adam spoke again. 'Did you...?' Adam sounded uncharacteristically hesitant. 'Did you try and resuscitate him?'

'Yes.'

'That must have been pretty rough.' Adam's dark eyes conveyed an empathy that Hannah could not afford to accept. Being close to him was painful enough without the knowledge that he cared.

'Yes,' she said curtly. They should have stuck to the weather after all.

'Do you still have nightmares?' Adam queried softly.

The movement of Hannah's head neither confirmed nor denied the suggestion. The turning to stare out of the side window passed on the clear message that the ground was now too personal. Adam no longer had any right to expect a reply.

The new silence was subdued. Adam could have no idea how close to the bone his intuition had struck. The nightmare had visited again only last night. But this time it had been different. Worse. Because this time she hadn't been able to tell whether the face of the man she had loved and lost had been that of Ben...or Adam. How had Adam slipped so easily and so completely under the guard she had erected around her heart? And how, in God's name, could she ever push him back to the other side?

'I shouldn't have asked.' Adam sounded apologetic. 'I know only too well that some things are best left buried.'

'Do you?' Hannah couldn't resist the opportunity to learn something more about Adam. Maybe if she knew more, she might be able to understand what had gone so wrong between them.

'I was married...briefly.' Adam's tone was guarded

now. 'Not for long. Not even long enough to get to know each other properly. My wife also died unexpectedly. And needlessly.'

'I'm sorry.' Hannah wanted to ask more questions. She glanced at Adam, trying to gauge how receptive he might be.

The glance sparked a sudden urge in Adam to tell Hannah everything, but the protective mechanisms were too well entrenched and too recently upgraded. He'd already said too much thanks to the startling revelation of Hannah's own tragedy. But that was as far as things would go. Hannah had been left with a lot more of her life—a lot more of herself intact than Adam had. Infinitely more. Adam shrugged.

'It's in the past,' he stated flatly. 'And that's exactly where it belongs.' He sighed. 'I shouldn't have asked,' he said again. 'I certainly wouldn't want anybody quizzing me.'

Hannah turned her gaze away. So Adam's personal areas were as out of bounds as hers now were. Fair enough. She had no right to expect anything more and any opportunity to try and regain the moment of contact ended as Adam pulled the vehicle to a halt outside the main entrance of the small maternity hospital.

'I'll get the ramps out,' Hannah offered quickly. 'We'll need them to load an incubator, won't we?'

Adam nodded. 'There's a bag of straps in the rear left locker. We'll need those as well to tie it in.'

The trip back to town was uneventful. A nurse travelled with the parents and baby to monitor the incubator settings and the condition of Baby Mulligan. There was nothing for Hannah to do but sit in the back. She eyed the impressive thatch of dark hair on the baby's tiny head.

Mrs Mulligan was very blonde, unlike her husband who had thick, black hair.

'I can see he's taking after his dad.' Hannah smiled.

The baby's mother nodded. 'He's pure Irish.'

'Have you decided on a name?'

The woman grinned. 'We've been calling him Paddy for the last eight months. It might stick. Especially seeing as it's his grandfather's name.'

'My daughter has Irish grandparents,' Hannah told her. She knew Adam could hear the conversation. 'I'm going to take her to Ireland to meet them one day.'

'Does she have black hair, too?'

'No.' Hannah picked up the end of her long braid. 'She took after me.' She flicked the braid back over her shoulder. 'At least she won't have to worry about going grey. Nobody will even notice the difference.'

It wasn't grey. It was silver. A shimmering shade that was absolutely unique. One out of the box. Like Hannah herself. Adam was acutely aware of his partner over the next few calls they had. She tackled anything, even a vomiting drunk, with the same competence, confidence and good humour. She had known the worst life could offer and yet she carried on, outwardly unscarred and prepared to go on living—and loving. Adam could imagine better than most what it had been like for her, trying to resuscitate her lover.

Maybe he should unlock his own doors and share the demons from his own past with another person for the first time. If he was ever going to share that pain with anyone, Hannah was the one person he would contemplate as a candidate. But it wasn't possible. He would be giving too much of himself away. If he did that he would become as vulnerable as he had ever been. And Hannah hadn't really known the worst that life could offer. She hadn't lost her child.

Maybe, given time, he would know whether he could place that amount of trust in another human. Maybe he would even be ready to risk everything he had clawed back from life in the last five years. Then again, maybe this was just a physical obsession. If he could get enough of Hannah for long enough, it might wear off. Then he would be able to get things back into perspective and he would be no worse off than he was now. A lot better off, in fact, because he could get rid of this obsession and the constant frustration of not being able to touch this woman. There had to be a way to compromise the situation he had created.

Adam didn't expect ninety-six-year-old Enid Packman to supply the catalyst for compromise. The call to the rest home came at 3 a.m. Adam was still trying to forget how deliciously rumpled Hannah had looked after emerging from her bedroom when they arrived at the Spring's Orchard Retirement Village to find a sprightly looking, tiny woman lying on top of her bed.

'What do you think, Hannah?'

'Where did you say the pain was, Miss Packman?'

'All down my leg, dear. It's dreadful, but only when I move.'

Hannah looked at their patient's stick-like legs. 'There's shortening on the left side,' she pointed out to Adam. 'And a marked internal rotation.' Miss Packman's right foot pointed straight up. The left foot was at a forty-five-degree angle, pointing inwards. 'I think she's probably fractured her left neck of femur.'

Adam nodded. 'We'll give her some pain relief and splint her legs with a pillow between them before we move her.' He patted Miss Packman's hand. 'What were you doing, to fall over at this time of night?'

'I got up to have breakfast, of course.' Miss Packman sounded indignant. 'Goodness knows why they want to serve breakfast in the middle of the night but I'm not one to make a fuss. I smelt the porridge so I got up. And then I fell over.' The old woman frowned reprovingly at the rest-home aide who was standing nearby. 'If you're going to serve breakfast at such an unreasonable time, the least you could do is put the lights on.'

Hannah was managing to contain her smile until she caught the wicked gleam in Adam's eye. The amusement was too much and she turned away quickly to let the grin escape.

Adam cleared his throat. 'How are you feeling right now, Miss Packman? Apart from the pain in your leg.'

'Cross,' declared their patient. 'And I'm hungry. I want my porridge.'

'You don't have any pains in your chest?' Adam persevered. They had been informed by the aide on their way in that Enid Packman had a cardiac history.

'No.' Enid's attention was on the aide again. 'Put some brown sugar and cream on mine, please. Only a little cream, though. It's bad for my heart.' She wagged her head at Adam. 'And I do have to watch my figure as well, of course.'

'Of course,' Adam agreed, openly smiling now. 'You look gorgeous, Enid. Now, I'm going to pop a wee needle in your hand and give you something for that pain in your leg. Then we'll take you for a drive to the hospital.'

'Do they have porridge there?'

'Buckets of it, I expect.' Adam clipped a tourniquet around Enid's arm. 'You're not allergic to anything that you know of, are you, Enid?'

'I don't like peanut butter.' Enid was watching Adam locate a vein in her hand. 'It sticks in my teeth.' She chuckled and leaned closed to Adam. 'Not that they're really *my* teeth, you know.'

Adam was grinning again. 'I meant medicines, Enid.' He looked at the aide. 'Any adverse reactions to anything ever noted?'

'No.' The young woman had also been enjoying Enid's conversation. 'There's no mention of any allergies in her records.'

'I'm allergic to men,' Enid informed Hannah. 'That's why I never got married.'

'Probably wise.' Hannah smiled.

'But, then, I never met anyone quite as nice as you.' Enid beamed at Adam. 'And so gentle, too. I hardly felt a thing.'

'I haven't put the needle in quite yet, Enid.' Adam was having difficulty not laughing aloud. 'Here we go.'

'I still didn't feel a thing,' Enid declared. 'Isn't he lovely? *Such* a nice man.'

The last comment was directed at Hannah who could only nod helplessly as she handed Adam the syringe of fluid to flush the line. Their gazes caught. Enid's effervescent personality and the humour she had unwittingly created had removed the last of the anger between Adam and Hannah. They shared a smile.

'Draw up nine mls of saline and one of morphine, would you, please, Hannah?' Adam requested. 'Let's see how comfortable we can make Enid before we try and move her.'

It was 4.30 a.m. before Unit 241 was available again. Enid Packman had been settled into the emergency department awaiting the arrival of an orthopaedic registrar. Her request for porridge had been regretfully declined by the emergency staff but Enid had been placated by the concern shown for her welfare.

'It's in case I need an anaesthetic,' she told Hannah. 'They don't want me to be sick. *Such* nice people, aren't they?'

Hannah was still smiling as they loaded the empty stretcher back into the ambulance. She reached for a crumpled blanket to refold it just as Adam had the same thought. Their hands brushed and Hannah backed off hurriedly. Stepping towards the front seat, Hannah remembered the paperwork she had left under the pillow. She turned to retrieve it just as Adam was moving forward. They collided.

'Sorry!'

'Don't be.' The husky note in Adam's voice caused Hannah to glance up swiftly. The eye contact then became impossible to break. 'I miss you,' Adam said softly.

'I miss you, too.'

Adam pushed his fingers through his hair and Hannah stared at the curl that now stood up like a duck's tail. 'It's very hard, working with you, Hannah.' Adam cleared his throat and then lowered his voice. 'Wanting you like this.' He sighed heavily. 'I thought it would wear off but I swear it's getting worse.'

Hannah said nothing. Instead, she slowly nodded her agreement.

'You feel the same way?' Adam asked very quietly. 'Really?'

Hannah lowered her gaze from the stray curl to Adam's eyes. Should she admit how strongly she felt? She probably couldn't hide it even if she said nothing. Certainly Adam seemed to read her answer in her face. He reached out one hand and gently stroked a finger down her cheek.

'What are we going to do, Hannah Duncan?'

'I don't know,' Hannah whispered. 'I don't think there's anything we *can* do.'

'There must be.' Adam's voice was stronger now. 'I don't think I can live like this. Without you in my life.'

'I am in your life.'

'You know what I mean.'

Hannah knew exactly what Adam meant. Her breath caught and she had to take a new one. 'We've got no future, Adam. You said so yourself.'

'We've got the present.'

Hannah shook her head imperceptibly. 'Is that all you really want, Adam? A relationship that's going nowhere? Just sex?'

'I could get "just sex" anywhere,' Adam told her impatiently. 'It's *you* I want.'

'I'm not alone,' Hannah reminded him. 'I've got a life and I'm not going to carve it up into separate boxes with one for you and one for my daughter.'

'I wouldn't expect you to.'

'What are you saying, Adam?' Hannah tried to quell the flash of hope. Maybe Adam was now prepared to try and accept her daughter. If he actually spent some time with Heidi, it was possible that his attitude towards children might change. Given time, it was even possible that he could do more that just accept her presence. He might even grow to love the small girl.

'I'm saying that I want to be with you.' Adam's expression was intense. 'The past is irrelevant. The future will take care of itself. What we have is here…and now.' The dim light and sense of privacy from being shut in the back of the vehicle accentuated the intimacy of the moment. Adam wasn't going to touch Hannah—not during working hours—but it was astonishingly difficult to try and convey his sincerity through words alone. 'The feelings I have for you are too strong to dismiss,' he said softly. 'And they're not going to go away. There has to be some way we can work through any problems we have. All I'm asking is that we try. Please,' he added.

Hannah's response was considered. It seemed to take a long time. 'I'd like that, Adam,' she said finally. A hint of a smile touched her lips. 'I think it's a very good idea.'

Adam smiled back. 'I think it might be the third best idea I've ever had.'

He started 241's engine and pulled away with more enthusiasm than the time of day warranted. He smiled at Hannah again and was rewarded with a definite echo of his own optimism. He didn't have to *marry* Hannah after all. He didn't even have to live with her, and how many women would want to drag their child out on too many dates? He probably wouldn't even see much of Heidi and when he did he could just employ the professional distance that served him so well on the job. He had dealt with hundreds of children and the technique had been honed to an art form. He could cope.

It was going to be easier than he'd expected. Heidi burst into tears the instant he stepped over the threshold into Hannah's home.

'Sorry.' Hannah gathered the wailing child into her arms. 'It's just that she's not used to strange men coming into the house.'

'She's as good as a burglar alarm.' Adam tried not to wince as Heidi turned up the volume at the sound of his voice.

'She's tired as well.' Hannah defended her daughter. 'I'll put her to bed in a minute.'

'I'll do that, if you like,' Norma offered. She was stand-

ing behind Adam, having been the one to answer the door-
bell.

'No—you get away, Mum. You don't want to be late
on a first date.'

Norma looked embarrassed. 'It's hardly a date. Gerry
just wanted some company for this GP evening.'

'Gerry Prescott is one of the doctors at the medical
centre Mum works for,' Hannah explained to Adam. 'He's
very nice,' she added with a smile at her mother, 'and
he's been trying to get Mum to go out with him for the
last two years.'

'I think the attraction is my family,' Norma suggested.
'Gerry didn't have children and he envies me my granddaughter. He adores Heidi as much as I do.'

'I hope you have a nice evening,' Adam told Norma
politely.

'It's just a drug company do,' Norma said offhandedly.
'We sit and listen to them talking about their products and
then get taken to a concert.' She moved to kiss the back
of Heidi's head. The toddler's face was still buried in
Hannah's neck. 'Bye, button.' Norma raised her eyebrows
at Hannah. 'Do I look all right?'

Hannah grinned. 'You look lovely. Go and have a good
time. I won't wait up for you.'

'I won't be late.' Norma nodded at Adam. 'Nice to see
you again, Adam.'

'And you, Norma.' Adam's smile was warm. 'I have
to agree with Hannah. You look lovely.' His smile broad-
ened. 'And very healthy, too.'

Norma returned the smile. 'I'll just find my walking
frame, then, and I'll be off.'

An awkward moment fell as soon as Norma had closed
the front door behind her. Hannah tried to put Heidi down

but the small girl wound her arms even more tightly around her mother's neck.

'No!' she announced.

Adam tried to look amused but the thought of Hannah eating dinner with him wearing her living necklace was somewhat offputting. Hannah must have caught the thought. She looked uncomfortable.

'There's a bottle of wine in the fridge,' she told Adam. 'Why don't you open it and pour us both a glass? I'll read Heidi her story and put her to bed.'

Adam waited a few minutes, sipping his glass of wine, but Hannah didn't appear in the kitchen. The delicious smell emanating from the oven gave Adam sharp hunger pangs so he wandered back into the living area. Evidence of a small child in residence was everywhere. A tiny table with matching chairs took up a corner of the room, with paper and crayons in a tidy pile on top. A basket of building blocks and a doll's house took up another corner. A well-nibbled and soggy-looking biscuit sat on the arm of the couch. It was the abandoned biscuit that caught a raw nerve for Adam.

Déjà vu. Maddy had never had time to finish her snacks before moving on to more interesting activities. The remains had always popped up in surprising and unwelcome places. Like the melted chocolate biscuit he'd found under his pillow one day. Or the carrot sticks floating in the toilet.

Adam moved into the hallway. He avoided the tiny tricycle and a large plastic beach ball. Hearing the soft murmur of Hannah's voice, he was drawn towards an open door near the bathroom.

'And the tiniest bear never lost its squeak ever again because there was always somebody there to hug him.'

'Queek *me*, Mumma!'

Adam paused in the doorway. He saw Hannah fold her arms around the child in her lap and instantly regretted his decision to leave the kitchen. The emotional tug was poignant enough to be physically painful. Adam took a large swallow from the glass he was still holding.

'You didn't queek me, Mumma.'

Hannah hugged her daughter again, this time adding a tickle that made the child squeal with delight. 'There, you squeaked.' Hannah smiled. 'Now it's time for bed.'

Adam stepped back as Hannah rose from the armchair. He didn't want her to think he'd been spying on her.

'Has the man gone home?'

Adam took another step back. Heidi's hopeful tone made it clear she was as wary of his company as he was of hers.

'Not yet, sweetheart,' he heard Hannah respond. 'The man is Mummy's friend. He's come to have dinner with me.'

'Me, too?'

'No.' This time Hannah sounded firm. Adam nodded approvingly as he headed back to the kitchen. He was topping up his glass of wine when Hannah appeared.

'Sorry, I didn't mean to take so long.'

'Not a problem,' Adam assured her. 'This is a very nice wine. I'm onto my second glass.'

'Thanks.' Hannah accepted the glass Adam was offering. 'Cheers.'

Adam's glance moved to roam the tiny galley kitchen they were standing in. 'This is a very interesting house,' he commented. 'I had a feeling you wouldn't fit into an apartment or a typical house in the suburbs.'

'These old terrace houses are unique,' Hannah agreed. 'They're so skinny. Just one room and a hallway all the way through. It's not ideal for Heidi because the back yard is too small, but we liked being central and we're only a stone's throw from the botanical gardens.'

'It has character,' Adam smiled. 'Buckets of it. You're nice and handy for the day centre as well.'

'Mmm.' Hannah didn't want to bring Heidi into the discussion too much.

'How's that little boy? The one we picked up with the elbow injury?' Adam sounded as though his interest was somewhat forced.

'He's fine. His mother painted Teletubbies on his cast and he thinks it's magic.' Hannah needed to steer the conversation in another direction. Talking to Adam about children wasn't a good idea. 'Are you hungry?'

'I didn't think so until I smelt whatever it is you have cooking.' Adam's relief at the change of topic was patent. He grinned at Hannah. 'All of a sudden I'm starving.'

'It's just a casserole,' Hannah said with a smile. 'Beef and mushrooms and a few other bits. Nothing special.'

'I can't cook for toffee,' Adam confessed, 'so it smells pretty special.' He touched his glass to Hannah's. 'Like you,' he added.

'Do I smell?' Hannah grinned.

'Let me see.' Adam took Hannah's glass away from her and put it down beside his. He scooped Hannah's loose hair back with both hands and bent his head to nuzzle her neck. 'You smell,' he announced thoughtfully as he straightened slowly, 'absolutely delicious.'

'Like casserole?' Hannah's eyes were fastened on his. Her face was very still.

'Like you.' Adam was still holding her hair. He bent his head again, this time to touch her lips with his own. He let the weight of hair drop free and threaded his fingers through the soft tresses to cradle her head. Hannah's lips parted beneath his and her hands came around his neck.

The taste of her mouth inflamed the desire Adam had been trying to keep in check for nearly two weeks. He pulled away finally with a frustrated growl.

'I think I'd better feed you.' Hannah sounded a little shaky.

'I know what I'd rather be eating,' Adam said wickedly.

Hannah flushed. 'We can't,' she said nervously. 'Not here.' The glance over her shoulder was an effective reminder that they weren't quite alone in the house. Adam managed a smile.

'It'll have to be casserole, then.' An eyebrow lifted suggestively. 'When would you like to come to my house for dinner? Tomorrow?'

'But you can't cook for toffee,' Hannah teased.

'There's always take-aways,' Adam countered. He lowered his voice and leaned towards Hannah. 'And who needs food, anyway?'

'We do,' Hannah said hurriedly. She stepped away and grabbed an oven glove. 'And right now—before we get distracted again.' She donned the glove and pulled the oven door open, before glancing back at Adam. 'Tomorrow sounds great,' she said shyly.

'I have good ideas,' Adam agreed. 'I'm beginning to like them a lot.'

Adam *did* have good ideas. It was Adam who suggested taking Heidi for a picnic at the beach on Thursday and to take both Heidi and Norma out for a pizza the following week. He alternated including Hannah's family in his ideas to capturing her time alone at his own house. Hannah's refusal to spend a full night away from home clearly disappointed Adam, and waiting for him to be ready to tell her more of his past frustrated Hannah. But everything considered, things were working out very well.

The fact that Adam was happy for their colleagues to know they were seeing each other had to be a step forward. Both Matt and Tom were outwardly delighted at the development. Heidi was still too shy to talk to Adam but he didn't appear to mind. Hannah suspected that he preferred the lack of interaction. At least Heidi didn't cry any more when he came to their house.

Hannah went through two more four-day working cycles before she found herself crewing with Adam again. She was now through the first two months of her probationary period. In a few weeks' time she would be heading back to the classroom for an intensive period of theoretical work with the exam for a Grade 1 qualification at the end of the study period.

'Are you going to be taking the Grade 1 class?' Hannah asked Adam.

'Fortunately not,' Adam responded.

'Why fortunately?'

'Because I'd have no chance of doing my job with you sitting in front of me all day, every day for three weeks.'

'You don't have any trouble doing your job when we're on the road together.'

'Want to bet?' Adam grinned over his shoulder. 'I've completely forgotten where we're even going right now.'

'Gibraltar Crescent,' Hannah reminded him. 'Sick person at number 209.' She consulted the map again. 'Take the next left and then the first on the right.'

'"Sick person" covers a nice wide range,' Adam mused. 'I wish we got a bit more information over the pagers sometimes. They must be busy up in Control.'

'Keeps life interesting,' Hannah pointed out. 'And it keeps us on our toes. We have to be ready for anything.'

The young woman that opened the door at number 209 did look like a sick person. She was very pale, her eyes looked sunken and she clutching her stomach, but she shook her head when Hannah asked what her problem was.

'It's not me I called you for,' she said miserably. 'It's my babies. Through here.'

Hannah remembered belatedly to introduce herself. 'I'm Hannah,' she told the woman as they followed her slow progress into another room. 'What's your name?'

'Susan.'

'You're not looking too well yourself, Susan.'

'It's just food poisoning or stomach flu or something.' Susan led the way into a living area. 'This is Molly and that's Tyler. They're a bit sick, too, and I can't get them to eat anything.'

Molly and Tyler were twins. About six months old, the babies lay on change mats on the floor. Both had been vomiting and smelt overdue for a nappy change. Both were crying loudly. Hannah bit her lip as she cast an apprehensive glance at Adam. He wasn't going to enjoy this call.

'Oh, God,' Susan groaned suddenly. ''Scuse me.' She turned and fled down the hall. Hannah and Adam could both hear the sound of her vomiting a few seconds later.

'Go and look after Susan,' Adam suggested. 'Lay her down for a few minutes when she's finished. Do some baseline observations and get a history. You could help her pack a few things for these two as well. I suspect they're getting dehydrated and their mother's in no condition to care for them. We'll have to take them all into hospital.'

'The babies need changing,' Hannah pointed out. 'I can do that.'

'Susan will need a wash and a clean nightie. I can't do

that,' Adam said. 'I'll deal with the babies. I'm not entirely useless.'

Hannah left Adam reluctantly. Susan had finally stopped vomiting and was now sitting on the bathroom floor, sobbing. Hannah found a clean towel and a face-cloth.

'It's going to be all right, Susan,' she assured her patient. 'I'll help you get cleaned up and lying down, and you'll feel a bit better.'

It took some time to sort out the twins' mother and help her to bed. Hannah took her blood pressure, pulse and respiration rate and quickly wrote out a history of the illness. 'We're going to take you into hospital,' she told Susan. 'Both you and the twins are getting dehydrated and it can be dangerous for babies.'

Susan nodded wearily. 'I didn't know what to do. I've been managing for the last two days but everything seemed so much worse this morning.'

'You did the right thing to call us,' Hannah told her. 'I'm going to pack some things for the twins. Have they got any clean stretch suits?'

'In the washing basket,' Susan nodded. 'I haven't put anything away for days. I'm sorry about the mess.'

'It's not important.' Hannah gave Susan's hand a quick squeeze as the tears began rolling down the young mother's face again. 'Where's the washing basket?'

'In the living room.'

The babies were still crying. Adam had gloves on and was washing Molly. Hannah edged past towards the washing basket.

'Throw us a clean nappy if there is one,' Adam requested.

Hannah obliged and was astonished to see Adam deftly

fold the square then apply it to the baby. 'Where did you learn to do that?' she asked in surprise.

Adam's smile was a trifle grim. 'I'm full of hidden talents,' he murmured. He eased the baby's legs into the clean stretch suit and snapped the buttons closed. 'OK.' He sighed heavily. 'Let's see if we can find the on-off switch, shall we?' He picked Molly up and put her over his shoulder, patting the baby's back. Molly's cries subsided almost instantly and her brother was left crying alone.

Hannah sorted quickly through the washing basket, pulling tiny garments to one side. She watched Adam steady Molly with one hand and reach over to Tyler.

'What's wrong, buddy? Clean trousers not enough for you?' He tickled the baby's stomach gently. 'You're a horrible child,' he said conversationally.

Hannah's eyes widened as Tyler stopped crying to grin at Adam. For someone who hated children, he certainly knew how to handle babies. Her curiosity resurfaced after they had transported the unwell threesome to Emergency. She eyed Adam as he climbed back into the driver's seat.

'Have you got lots of brothers or sisters or something?'

'No, I'm an only child. Why?'

'I thought maybe you had a whole bunch of nieces and nephews. You seem to know what you're doing with babies.' Her eyes narrowed speculatively. 'It's not something that comes naturally, you know. Particularly for men.'

Adam shrugged. 'I've been doing this job for a long time. We do get to handle babies occasionally.' He pulled away from the ambulance bay. 'Let's see if we can get as far as headquarters and find a coffee before they find any more undersized specimens of sick people for us.'

Hannah made a sound of general agreement but her

thoughts were still elsewhere. Adam wasn't fooling her. Handling babies and children on the job could never lead to enough experience to explain the ease Adam had just demonstrated. Back at headquarters Hannah went to the women's toilets to give her hands another thorough wash. She was hoping that neither she nor Adam had picked up any nasty gastric virus. As she dried her hands, the door opened to admit Katherine Gordon, one of the few female staff members. On Red shift, Katherine's path didn't cross Hannah's very often, but she knew the older woman well enough to enjoy her company.

'I hear you and Adam just dealt with a minor epidemic,' Katherine grinned. 'Sounded ghastly.'

'I'm sure Adam made it sound much worse than it actually was.'

'I'm sure he did,' Katherine agreed. 'He loves to hate babies.'

Hannah dropped the paper towels into the waste bin. 'I'm beginning to have my doubts about that,' she commented. 'I don't think Adam *really* hates babies at all.'

'Course he doesn't.' Katherine pushed open the door of a cubicle. 'I've worked with him long enough to know he's as soft as they come.' She disappeared behind the door but her voice floated out. 'For some reason he just doesn't want anyone to know and he puts up a good enough front to fool the men.'

Hannah found herself staring at Adam as she stirred her cup of coffee. Her love for this man had grown so much stronger over the last few weeks. She didn't want to imagine a future without him but a niggle of disquiet persisted. What if he never accepted Heidi? If his dislike of children was a public front for whatever reason, then it didn't bode well for their relationship if she—and Heidi—were being kept on the same side of the fence as everybody else.

Adam still hadn't said anything more about his brief and apparently tragic marriage. Hannah had shared her own past—had tried to give Adam the opportunity to reciprocate without appearing to be 'quizzing' him, but Adam always managed to sidetrack with practised ease. Maybe Adam had wanted children once. His *wife's* children. Had the loss left him too bitter to contemplate the same future with someone else? Or maybe he hadn't found someone who measured up quite well enough yet. Was the problem that Adam didn't want to hurt her feelings by telling her that?

Hannah had barely sipped her coffee before her pager buzzed. A priority-one call to someone having breathing difficulties. Hannah gave up on her personal worries as she moved quickly back to the garage. She was confident that, given time, things would sort themselves out. Hadn't Adam himself said that the past was irrelevant and the future would take care of itself? Life was too good right now to risk rocking the boat.

Life was great right now. Adam had it pegged. He was seeing Hannah almost as often as he wanted and it just got better as time went on. That was a bit of a worry, in fact. Adam had expected his feelings for her to be wearing off about now. Or at least settling down to a point where he didn't feel let down when Hannah left his bed to go home before morning. Or jealous because she wanted to spend a day alone with her daughter. Or even irritated by the length of time it took to drive from his suburb to hers. Adam was beginning to resent the time he spent away from Hannah's company. It felt like marking time, wasting hours they could have spent together. He found himself wondering whether it might not be such a silly idea to contemplate living together.

Having Heidi around wasn't so bad. Admittedly she was a cute kid but she hadn't wormed her way past the emotional guard Adam had reinforced. He almost enjoyed her company now that she wasn't quite so shy. He could see a lot of Hannah in the child, which was rather intriguing, but Adam wouldn't be devastated if Heidi simply vanished in a puff of smoke. It was Hannah he wanted and if spending time with Heidi was the price he had to pay then Adam was more than willing to meet the cost.

A trip to the botanical gardens had been arranged for Saturday afternoon, after Adam had learned that the playground was one of Heidi's favourite destinations. Hannah was supposed to have made a picnic afternoon tea for them all, but when Adam arrived she had nothing ready.

'I'm sorry,' Hannah apologised. 'I'm not feeling great.'

'What's wrong?' Adam asked, more sharply than he'd intended. The concern he felt was surprisingly intense.

'I think I've got a touch of whatever those twins had,' Hannah said mournfully. 'I've thrown up three times in the last half hour.'

'Sit down,' Adam ordered. 'You don't look good.' Hannah was very pale. 'Is Heidi sick, too?'

'No. She's bouncing around.' Hannah put her hands over her face. 'I keep wanting to fall asleep but I can't because she needs watching.'

'Where's Norma?'

'Gone for a long bike ride with Gerry Prescott.' Hannah smiled wanly. 'She's feeling fine as well. I hope I don't pass this on.'

'Go and lie down,' Adam told Hannah. 'And have a sleep. You'll feel much better.'

'But I can't,' Hannah protested.

'Yes, you can,' Adam insisted. 'I'll look after Heidi. In

fact…' Adam surprised even himself as he spoke '…I'll take her to the playground myself. That way you'll get some peace and quiet for an hour or two.'

Hannah's jaw dropped slightly. 'Are you sure you want to do that, Adam?'

Heidi came running into the kitchen, dragging a wooden buzzy-bee toy. The wings clattered loudly and Hannah buried her face again. She was clearly too tired and unwell to put up much of a protest at the noise level. Adam crouched down.

'Heidi, do you want to come to the playground with me?'

'And Mumma?' Heidi tugged at Hannah's elbow.

'No, just with me.'

Heidi stuck her thumb in her mouth. Adam had become used to the signal that she didn't want to talk to him any more.

'Mummy's not feeling well,' Adam persisted. 'She needs to have a sleep while you and I go to the gardens. And have a swing,' he added craftily.

Wide blue eyes studied Adam carefully. The thumb came out of Heidi's mouth only when a decision had been made. 'OK,' Heidi agreed. 'Swing now.'

'Soon,' Adam promised. 'Let's find your coat just in case the sun decides to have a sleep as well. I'm going to take Mummy to bed.'

Hannah managed another wan smile. 'Watch what you're saying in front of my daughter.'

Adam grinned. 'Chance would be a fine thing. Don't worry, I prefer my women a bit healthier than you are right now. I'll tuck you up and make you a cup of tea. You probably need something for that headache as well.'

Hannah steadied herself on the table as she rose. 'How did you know I had a headache?'

'You didn't exactly greet the arrival of Buzzy Bee with any enthusiasm.' Adam put a hand on Hannah's elbow. 'Come on. Off to bed.'

Heidi insisted on taking Buzzy Bee to the gardens. They were within walking distance and the toy clacked merrily as Heidi dragged it along the footpath behind her. When they came to a road to cross, Heidi automatically stuck her hand in the air and Adam, just as automatically, took hold of it. The last time he had held a child's hand while crossing a road had been the day he'd taken Maddy to day care for the last time. Adam had to grit his teeth for at least a minute and remind himself very firmly that this wasn't Maddy. It was Heidi. Someone else's child that he had only a temporary responsibility for.

The playground was busy and Heidi had to wait for a turn on the swings. Then she wanted to climb through the tunnels, build a sand castle and have another swing. Adam found the bustle of children's activity and the noise level exhausting. He was more than ready to head home after an hour.

'No,' Heidi declared. 'Want to play.'

'Five more minutes,' Adam directed. 'Then we'll go and find an ice cream.'

'OK.' Heidi turned and made her way to the climbing frame. She stepped up one rung and hung there, her head tilted, exchanging glances with a small boy on the other side. Adam stood beside her, holding Buzzy Bee's string. He turned as an elderly woman spoke to him.

'What a delightful little girl you have.'

'She's not mine,' Adam felt obliged to point out. 'I'm just babysitting.'

'Well, she's lovely. How old is she?'

'Two and a half.'

'I'm here with my grandson. He's in the sand pit.'

Adam followed the woman's gaze to where a sand-throwing fight was in progress.

'Oh, dear.' The woman moved off. 'William! Stop that this minute!'

Adam turned back. Heidi had vanished. The realisation took several heartbeats to sink in. With dawning horror, Adam's head swivelled. She was nowhere near the swings. Had she crawled into one of the solid tunnels again? God, he'd only looked away from her for a second. The playground was full of children, all of whom seemed to be moving at high speed. Adam's rapid scanning failed to lock onto anyone remotely resembling Heidi but he called out anyway.

'Heidi! Where are you?'

'Here.' The piping voice was unmistakable.

Adam looked up. Heidi was now on the top of the climbing frame, well above his head height. She had turned to look down at him and Adam swallowed hard. How the hell had she managed that? And why had anybody been allowed to build a structure that high in a public playground?

'Come down here at once,' Adam snapped.

'OK,' Heidi said obligingly. She let go of the metal rung she was holding and jumped.

Adam hadn't known his reactions were quite that fast. He caught the tiny girl in his arms and the shock of what had just happened kicked in a second later.

'You *naughty* girl,' he growled. 'That was a *stupid* thing to do.'

Heidi's face crumpled as she caught the fear Adam had experienced. She began to cry with heartbroken sobs and Adam took a deep breath.

'It's all right,' he said more calmly. 'But you must never, ever do that again. You might get hurt.'

Heidi's sobs intensified. Feeling the stare of other adults and children, Adam bent and retrieved Buzzy Bee's string without letting go of Heidi. He moved to a vacant park bench at the side of the playground. He couldn't take Heidi home in this state. What would Hannah think?

The small, tousled blonde head was buried against Adam's shoulder. He could feel the dampness of her tears on his neck. Adam sat and patted Heidi's back. Comforting noises came from a memory bank he had retired long ago. The sobs slowed down and finally stopped. Adam lapsed into silence, easing his burden into a more comfortable position. He tried not to think about how it felt to be holding a child in his arms again. Unaware of how much time had passed, Adam was startled to find that Heidi had fallen asleep in his arms.

The tiny face was upturned, the last trace of tears gone. Adam debated waking Heidi but she looked too peaceful to disturb for the moment. A perfect little face. The upset that her leap of faith had caused was completely erased. Adam's smile was wistful. Heidi *had* trusted that he would catch her. That he would be there to ensure that no harm came to her. And he had been, thank God. She was safe and she would trust him again. Before he realised what he was doing, Adam bent his head to plant a soft kiss on the child's forehead. Heidi's eyelids fluttered and then opened. The wide, blue eyes took a moment to focus and then Heidi's lips curved into a smile.

Adam smiled back. He let Heidi climb off his lap and tried to ignore the empty feeling in his arms.

'Go home?' Heidi queried brightly.

Adam nodded. Heidi smiled again and held up her hand. As Adam felt the tiny fingers curl trustingly around his own he knew he was lost. Heidi had done what he had sworn never to let another child do. She had won his love.

The fear Adam had experienced when Heidi had launched herself off the climbing frame paled in comparison to the emotion he was now forced to recognise. The fear of losing a child that now meant as much to him as her mother did. He loved them both.

Adam couldn't cope with that at all.

CHAPTER SEVEN

SOMETHING was bothering Adam.

Hannah thought it was unlikely that the cause of his withdrawal was the priority-one call they had just responded to for a traffic accident. Adam must have been to hundreds of traffic accidents by now. Besides, he'd seemed preoccupied ever since they'd started their day shift together and that was many hours ago now.

The traffic on the one-way system was parting ahead of them as though a giant broom was clearing a path. A van was slow to pull to one side and Adam gave a resounding blast on the air horn. The driver's gesture was unappreciative as they flashed past.

'Do you want a map reference?' Hannah raised her voice. The siren seemed even louder than usual today.

Adam shook his head. 'The Ngauranga Gorge road—just north of the quarry turn-off. We can't miss it.'

The radio was barely audible. Hannah just caught their unit number and signalled Adam as she picked up the microphone. She depressed the side button.

'Unit 241. Go ahead, Control.'

Static cut off the first part of the message. 'Truck and trailer unit rolled at the bottom of the hill. It appears to have collected up to three oncoming cars.'

Adam flicked the siren off. 'What about backup?'

Hannah depressed the button again. 'Any indication of casualty numbers?' she queried.

'Negative,' Control responded. 'Possibly upwards of

four. Two status-one patients according to a witness. Some are trapped. Code 100 responding.'

Hannah glanced at Adam. Status-one patients were critical. They were unconscious, could be having difficulty breathing or might have uncontrolled haemorrhage. Code 100 was the fire service who would be needed to cut any trapped victims from their vehicles. This sounded like a serious incident.

'What about backup?' Adam repeated.

Hannah relayed the query.

'Unit 225 backing you. City medic is also responding.'

Adam nodded and turned the siren back on. He put his foot down and moved to the centre of the road. Oncoming vehicles were forced to move aside as well as those they were passing on their side of the road. Hannah held her breath for a second as they went between two buses. Adam's pace, if anything, increased.

'Unit 241, do you copy?'

Hannah hastily pressed the microphone key again. 'Roger!'

A glance in the large side mirror showed Hannah more flashing lights well behind them. It was probably the city medic who drove a stationwagon-type car. As the station manager, he only participated in calls when staff numbers were down and the call was serious enough to require more than one paramedic. Hannah transferred her gaze to the windscreen, not daring to look at the speedometer. She had never travelled this fast in her life.

She had also never been to a major car crash. It was the image conjured up instantly when people thought of ambulances but in reality it wasn't a common job. Adam was concentrating on getting them there as quickly as possible. Hannah was concentrating just as hard—trying to remember all she had been taught. What would be the first thing to do when faced with such a serious situation? SRABC. The learned steps were there readily enough. Scene size-up and safety. Responsiveness of patient. Airway, breathing and circulation. The things to assess and the order in which to do them. Theory was always so different to reality, however. What might they find in the scene size-up? Downed power lines? Spilt fuel and a potential fire hazard? What had the truck and trailer been carrying? Toxic materials, possibly. And what if they had more than one critically injured and unresponsive patient? Would Hannah be expected to deal with someone by herself?

Hannah found the palms of her hands were damp as she clenched her fists nervously.

'Are you all right?'

Hannah hadn't noticed Adam looking at her. 'I'm fine.'

'You look pale.' Adam overtook another bus. The fast lane ahead was clear. 'I'm not sure you're well enough to be at work today.'

'I feel fine,' Hannah assured him. 'I spent Sunday and Monday in bed and took things quietly yesterday. I'm completely recovered.'

'You still look pale.'

'I've never been to a major car accident,' Hannah admitted. 'I'm just a bit nervous.'

'You'll be fine. Just remember your ABCs.'

Hannah nodded. They were entering the main motorway system out of the central city area now and traffic was less of a problem.

'That's better,' Adam declared. He increased their speed and flashed Hannah a speculative glance which she answered with a reassuring smile. It was nice that Adam still had time to be concerned about her welfare. Perhaps it was that concern which had made him appear preoccupied today. Right now they both needed to focus on the accident scene they would encounter within the next few minutes.

Despite the noise of their own siren Hannah could hear another emergency vehicle following them. A police car overtook the ambulance and quickly pulled ahead. Hannah checked the glovebox for the reflective yellow waistcoat she would need to wear at an accident scene. She also pulled two pairs of gloves from the box on the floor, handing one pair to Adam before donning hers.

Hannah ran a quick mental checklist of where everything they might need was kept in the ambulance in case she had to find something in a hurry. Items such as the suction kit, oxygen, neck collars and defibrillator were easy. She had to think harder about body splints and the anti-shock trousers. And would she remember how a scoop stretcher fitted together? Surprisingly, Hannah's nervousness vanished as they finally approached the scene. Adam would know exactly what to do. She was his partner and as a team, they would be able to cope with anything.

The scene wasn't as chaotic as Hannah had feared, though it had been tricky weaving through the rapidly building traffic jam as they neared their destination. The truck and trailer unit lay on its side, blocking much of the highway. The police had stopped traffic moving near the scene in both directions. One car lay on its roof, half in a ditch at the side of the motorway. Another had its bonnet crushed under the trailer unit of the huge truck. A third car was on the other side of the road, its side caved in by the telegraph pole which had stopped its spin. Several people were standing on the road. One woman was sitting, slumped, with her head in her hands.

Adam drew slowly to a halt, having scanned the scene

carefully. The city medic's car pulled up alongside them and another police car arrived. Emergency personnel were taking over the scene.

Ivan Moresby, the station manager, was rapidly fielding information from both bystanders and police as Adam and Hannah joined the group. Ivan nodded towards Adam.

'No sign of the fire crews yet but they shouldn't be far away. You and Hannah check out the car in the ditch. Apparently there's at least one conscious patient in there. Sounds like we have two status zeros in the car under the trailer but I'll just go and confirm that.'

Adam and Hannah moved quickly towards the side of the road. The woman sitting in their path had apparently been the sole occupant of the third vehicle involved in the accident. A very rapid assessment showed them that the woman was having no difficulty breathing and wasn't bleeding badly. Adam took the few seconds needed to apply a cervical collar and a policewoman was deployed to stay with the woman until another ambulance crew arrived. Adam and Hannah both needed to assess the occupants of the car in the ditch.

A male bystander climbed out of the ditch as they approached. He looked distressed, which was understandable. They could all hear the frantic cries for help coming from the car.

'The doors are all jammed, mate,' the man told Adam. 'There's no way to get in.'

Hannah could hear the high-pitched cry of a very young child beneath the feminine sobbing now punctuating the shouts. Crouching down to peer through the back window of the car, she could see a child's car seat and the dangling small legs. The child's head was hidden by the padded sides of the restraint. Hannah tried the buckled doorhandle to no avail.

Adam was moving around the front of the car to try the passenger door. The woman was now shrieking hysterically.

'Don't go! Please, don't go! *Get us out!*'

Hannah moved to put her face close to the front window. 'We'll get you out as soon as we can,' she called. 'Try not to move at the moment.'

'My baby. Please, save my baby!'

'The back window's open a fraction,' Adam told Hannah. 'I'm going to try and force it down.' He looked past Hannah, his face creased anxiously. 'The fire service should be here any minute.'

Hannah was trying to assess the woman's condition. She was hanging upside down, held by her safety belt. Her hair hung loose, trailing on the ceiling of the car which was streaked with blood. She was talking, groaning and crying non-stop so couldn't be having too much difficulty with her breathing. Her arms and hands were moving but her legs appeared caught under the bent steering assembly. Wide, horrified eyes were fastened on Hannah.

'What's your name?' Hannah called.

'Trudy.'

'I'm Hannah.' Hannah smiled. 'Does it hurt you to breathe at all, Trudy?'

'No—I don't think so. I just want to get *out* of here.' Trudy started crying again.

'I know you do, love. We're just waiting for the fire department to arrive. They'll have all the gear needed to cut this door open. Do you have any pain in your neck?'

'I don't know,' Trudy sobbed. 'Everything hurts. Except my legs.'

'Can you feel your legs?'

'No.' Trudy's arms moved as she tried to pull herself

upright. She collapsed back into her original position. 'My legs are stuck,' she moaned. 'I can't move.'

Hannah searched for some way to reassure the young mother. The wail of another approaching siren helped. 'That's the fire engine,' Hannah called through the window. 'They'll have you out of here in no time, I expect.'

'My baby,' Trudy wailed. *'Please…'*

Hannah had been watching Adam's attempts to force the back window open. He succeeded just as the baby's renewed cries reminded Trudy of her overwhelming concern. Now she could see Adam leaning into the car, stretching his arm to try and reach the catch on the safety belt holding the child restraint. His hand fumbled blindly, missing its target by a couple of inches. Hannah straightened.

'Let me try,' she called. 'I'm smaller than you are.' Hannah reached the far side of the car by the time Adam had pulled himself clear. Ivan Moresby was approaching them.

'Both status zero in the first car,' he informed them.

Hannah blinked in dismay. Status zero signified a fatality. With a quick glance at Adam, she knelt down and eased the front half of her body as far as she could through the open window space.

'What's the position here?' Ivan enquired.

'Driver is Trudy. She's status three. No breathing difficulties or major bleeding. She's trapped under the steering-wheel and the door is jammed so we can't get in to her. There's a baby in a car seat in the back. We're just trying to get close enough to assess it now.'

Hannah could feel the warmth of the baby's body and could see a bright red face. She stretched further and reached over the other side of the bucket seat to try and locate the safety belt catch.

'I can smell fuel,' Ivan said suddenly.

'Where the hell is code 100?' Adam growled. 'I heard their siren minutes ago.'

'They're having trouble getting through the traffic snarl. The police are having to clear the way.' Ivan stooped to peer through the driver's window. 'Hello, Trudy!' he called. 'We'll have you out as soon as we can. Do you know whether your car is fitted with an airbag?' He straightened quickly at Trudy's response, catching Adam's eye.

'Did you hear that?' he asked quietly.

Adam nodded tersely as he experienced a moment of real fear. Not for himself but for the woman now lying half into the battered vehicle. He touched Hannah's back.

'Come away, Hannah. This isn't safe.'

'Just a sec.' Hannah's fingers scrabbled for the button to release the safety belt. 'I've almost got it.'

'I'll go and intercept the fire crew,' Ivan decided. 'We're going to need a cover for that airbag before we can touch anything.'

Adam watched Ivan move away. Trudy's distressed cries were suddenly more unnerving. An undeployed airbag could trigger at any moment up until an hour after the impact. The electronic activity could cause an explosion if there was a fuel leak. He hadn't smelt petrol when they'd first approached but he could smell it now. And Hannah was *inside* the car.

'*Now*, Hannah!' Adam put his hands around her waist to pull her clear.

'I've got it,' Hannah shouted. 'I just need to turn it sideways so we can get it through the window.'

Hannah's body slithered backwards. The handle of the car seat caught on the window-frame. Hannah depressed the side buttons and folded the handle back. The baby was about four months old and felt heavy. Hannah was glad of Adam's support as she pulled herself to her feet, still clutching the car seat.

'Move,' Adam said tensely.

Hannah hadn't been aware of the conversation about the airbag. She stared at Adam in momentary confusion. Adam took hold of her arm firmly and pulled her away. He could see the fire engine coming to a halt, having edged past their ambulance. He could hear the frantic cries of the baby's mother as they left her further behind, with Adam towing Hannah as quickly as he could.

Adam heard the warning shout from one of the fire crew now approaching at a run, a safety cover for an undeployed airbag dangling from his hand. Adam turned to see even their limited view of the car's driver obscured by the inflating airbag. The fireman had reached Hannah's other side. He turned abruptly and put an arm across her back, his heavy jacket shielding both her and the baby she was carrying. The sound of Trudy's screams was cut off abruptly by the airbag. The sudden silence was shocking but couldn't prepare them for what came next. The explosion itself was quite muted but the shock wave was enough to make Hannah stumble. Both Adam and the fire officer caught her. She was still gripping the handle of the car seat fiercely. She turned with the others to see the spiral of flames and black smoke enveloping the car.

Hannah twisted free of the arms that held her. *'Oh, my God!'* She put the car seat down on the ground, ready to run as she straightened. Not to safety. Hannah intended to run back towards the car. Adam caught her and held her hard.

'There's nothing you can do, Hannah.' He turned her towards himself and held her in his arms, trying to shield her view. 'I'm afraid there isn't anything any of us can do.'

There was frantic activity around the fire engine as its crew swung into action, but the sudden and vicious fire had done its damage by the time it was under control. Adam had directed Hannah into the back of their ambulance and kept her busy assessing the baby. The second ambulance, crewed by Tom and Derek, had arrived. They dealt with the woman in the neck collar. Ivan had returned to headquarters. There was little more to do at the scene.

The baby's colour had quickly returned to normal once the infant had attained an upright position. The safety harness and padding inside the seat seemed to have protected it from any injury. Hannah was holding the child in her arms now and it lay quietly, one tiny hand clutching the end of Hannah's long silver braid. Hannah was staring through the tinted, narrow, back windows of the ambulance. She was watching the burnt-out vehicle, now being screened by tarpaulins. The baby's mother, Trudy, was still trapped inside.

Adam opened the back door at a knock. The policewoman they had spoken to earlier looked subdued.

'The baby's father has been traced. He'll meet you at the hospital.'

Adam nodded. 'Thanks. Did you get a name?'

'Freeman. The father is John. The baby is Melissa.'

'We'll get going, then.'

It was the policewoman's turn to nod. She turned away and Adam's mouth twisted in sympathy. They would be at the scene a lot longer and the work to be done now was grim.

Hannah was aware that she should return baby Melissa to the safety seat for the trip back into the city, but she couldn't bring herself to release the comforting warmth of the small body. The baby tugged on her plait and smiled. Hannah found herself perilously close to tears.

'Sit on the stretcher,' Adam said rather gruffly. 'I'll strap you both in and you can keep holding her.'

Adam drove slowly back into the city. Frequent glances in the rear-view mirror showed him the back of Hannah's head, bent protectively over the bundle in her arms. A heavy weight settled over him, threatening his concentration. Adam tried to push it away, dismayed at the effect the job was having. He had coped with worse than this. The protective shell he had developed to encase himself on a personal level had had a flow-on effect on his work.

Adam kept his eyes on the road, braking for a red light as they entered the one-way system into the central city. He knew what the problem was. The cracks in the shell had been obvious enough even before this distressing case. Cracks which his feelings for Hannah and now her child had caused. The fear he had felt for Hannah when she had been in danger had pushed one of those cracks even wider. The thought of not having pulled Hannah clear before that explosion had occurred was enough to send a cold shudder right through Adam's body.

'All right back there?' Adam needed to check.

'We're fine.' Hannah's voice was distant. She sounded anything but fine.

Adam sighed as he accelerated again. A new fear was presenting itself. What if he allowed the shell to crack enough to fall away? Allowed himself to love—and be loved again. It wouldn't be just a personal risk he was taking. He would become far too vulnerable to the stresses this job was capable of producing. Stresses such as to-day's case had displayed. It was all right for people who had never experienced a devastating loss. Sympathy was very different to empathy. Even empathy could be very different to knowing just how deep that black hole could be. Adam wasn't strong enough to take that on board voluntarily. Nobody was.

Tom and Derek had reached the emergency department and handed over their patient before Adam and Hannah arrived. They were watching Hannah as she carried the baby through the automatic doors. Their expressions conveyed concern. Hannah tried to smile but failed miserably. Even Derek had been through major incidents such as this during his career as a police officer. It was only Hannah who was struggling—wondering how she had ever thought she could cope with this job.

Hannah handed the baby to the triage nurse.

'The baby's father is in one of the side rooms,' the nurse told them. 'He'd like to talk to someone about the accident.'

Hannah's frightened gaze caught Adam's. He touched her arm lightly. 'I'll do this.'

Hannah nodded mutely. She watched them walk through the department. Her own strength seemed to be deserting her. It was moving further away with every step Adam took. Tom and Derek responded to another call and Hannah found herself standing alone near the doors to the ambulance bay. She returned to the back of the vehicle and sat down on the stretcher.

Burying her face in her hands, Hannah sat very still for what seemed like a long time. She uncovered her face but didn't look up when she heard the back door open and then close again. The stretcher mattress dipped as Adam settled himself beside her. He put an arm around her shoulders and Hannah allowed herself the luxury of turning her face into his shoulder.

'Sorry.' Her voice was muffled. 'I'm not going to make

a very good ambulance officer if I fall apart like this, am I?'

'You're not falling apart.' Adam squeezed her shoulder gently. 'You're having a perfectly normal reaction to a very stressful incident. A lot of people would have more trouble coping than you are. That's why we have debriefing procedures and counselling available.' Adam stroked the back of Hannah's head. 'You saved that baby. If I'd known about the airbag I wouldn't have even let you try until the wheel had been secured. We would have lost them both.'

Hannah nodded slowly. That would have been unbearable—to know that a baby had been trapped in that burning car. Suddenly, more than anything, Hannah wanted to go home. To hold her own child.

'Does it get any easier?' she asked Adam quietly. 'To deal with things like this?'

'You learn to distance yourself,' Adam responded. 'You have to, or you don't survive. That doesn't mean you have to become hard, though.' Adam took a deep breath and tightened his grip on Hannah for a second. Was that what was happening to him? What he wanted to happen? Right now what Adam wanted more than anything was to tell Hannah of his fears and the reasons for them. She would understand. If he *could* tell her, maybe something would change. For the better. Adam grasped the hope with determination. He *would* tell her. But not here.

'We'll have a debriefing to go to later,' he told Hannah.

'What happens?' Hannah didn't sound enthusiastic.

'Everyone involved in the incident gets together. We talk about it and our reactions to it. Ivan will probably call in a professional counsellor or psychologist to run the session.'

'Do we have to go?' Hannah didn't like the idea of exposing herself emotionally to people she didn't know.

'It's advisable but not compulsory.'

'I'd rather just talk to you.'

Adam smiled. 'I'd like to talk to you, too,' he said softly. '*Really* talk.' He touched Hannah's cheek with his forefinger. 'Come home with me tonight.'

Hannah straightened up with a sigh. 'I can't, Adam. Mum's got a class tonight. She won't be able to babysit.'

'Can't she miss one evening?'

Hannah chewed her lip. 'She's learning to make stained-glass windows. She's making one for the bathroom and she's going to finish it tonight. It's the final class.'

'Don't you have any other babysitters?'

Hannah shook her head slowly. She wanted to tell Adam that there was no way in the world she would be separated from her own daughter. Not tonight. But Adam's need for her was strong enough to taste. She couldn't push him away in favour of her daughter. Especially not after today.

'Come home with me,' she suggested evenly. 'I'll get Heidi into bed early and Mum will be out until ten. Unless…' Hannah trailed into silence. Unless Adam was interested in something more than talking. Unless having Heidi in the house had become too much of an unwelcome obstacle for Adam.

Adam saw her expression change. He could see the direction of her thoughts. As much as he craved holding Hannah and making love to her to reaffirm their own existence and bond, there was a more important intimacy they could achieve tonight.

'I'll bring dinner.' He smiled. 'I'll be there at 7 p.m.'

*   *   *

Adam arrived exactly on time. Hannah opened the door and ushered him through to the living room.

'Sit down,' she invited hurriedly. 'I'll get you a drink.'

'Perhaps I'd better put these in the oven first.' Adam held out the paper bags he was carrying.

'I'll take them.' Hannah reached quickly for the package but her hand slipped as she tried to get a grip on the hot foil-lined bag. Fortunately, Adam hadn't let go.

'Maybe *you* should sit down,' he suggested. 'And I'll get *you* a drink.'

Hannah laughed nervously. 'Sorry.' Adam's gaze was too focused. Too concerned. 'I guess I am a bit stressed.'

'Sit,' Adam ordered with an understanding smile. 'I'll be right back.'

Hannah obediently sat, choosing a chair near the fireplace. The half hour she had been home had wound her up far more than she'd realised. Her joy at being with her daughter again had been tinged with irritation. It hadn't helped that Norma had chosen today to buy the bed they'd been planning to get for Heidi. The small girl's shrill excitement at the tangible evidence of a new maturity had grated on Hannah's need for some quiet reassurance. She'd listened to Heidi's gleeful shrieks as Norma had bathed her while she herself had had her shower and changed out of her uniform. Even Norma had seemed a little rattled.

'I hope she goes to sleep before Adam gets here.' Norma had left herself with only just enough time to get to her evening class.

'It won't matter if she doesn't. I think Adam accepts that Heidi is part of the deal now, Mum.'

'Do you?' Norma was searching the pockets of her anorak for her car keys. The look she cast distractedly at Hannah was worrying.

'Don't you?' Hannah frowned. Norma had been the only one to see Adam when he had returned from the park with Heidi on Saturday. Hannah had been sound asleep. Norma had also fielded the phone calls from Adam over the next few days. Hannah remembered how preoccupied Adam had seemed earlier today. A puzzle piece suddenly fell into a place she would rather not have found.

'Found them,' Norma exclaimed in relief. 'I'm off, then.'

'You don't think he does, do you, Mum?' Hannah couldn't let her mother disappear just yet. This could be important.

'I'm sure he does,' Norma said quickly. Too quickly.

Hannah's look was enough to let Norma know that she couldn't get away with the glib reassurance. 'It's just that he seemed in rather a hurry to get home on Saturday, that's all, love. I got the impression that he found looking after Heidi by himself a bit much.'

'Well, he won't be by himself tonight.' Hannah smiled with relief as her mother escaped. Of course Adam might have found a solo effort disconcerting. She knew it hadn't done any harm, however. Not from her point of view, anyway. Heidi had been talking about Adam ever since. Her reticence over having a man in her house was definitely a thing of the past, but Hannah hadn't told her that Adam was coming tonight. Maybe Adam wouldn't share Hannah's delight that Heidi had accepted him. It was something that needed careful handling. Particularly in Adam's case.

The fact that Heidi's blue eyes were still sparkling as Hannah tucked her into the new bed, flanked by her favourite toys, only moments before Adam's arrival added to Hannah's disquiet. Too much that needed thinking about had happened today.

Thank goodness Adam seemed to be taking everything in his stride. He knew how to cope and would be able to help Hannah put things into perspective. They had each other, she and Adam. They had saved a baby today and her own precious daughter was alive and happy. Hannah took a deep, calming breath and was able to smile at Adam with genuine pleasure as she accepted her glass of wine. Adam sat down in the other armchair, facing Hannah.

The small, excited face at the living room door attracted Hannah's attention instantly.

'Oh, no,' she murmured. Heidi's eyes looked even brighter now that she had discovered she could get out of bed by herself. She carried her teddy bear and had her thumb stuck into her mouth, but she wasn't looking for her mother. Heidi's gaze was firmly on Adam. She pulled her thumb free.

''Lo, man,' she announced.

Adam jumped visibly. With his back half-turned towards the door, he had been unaware of Heidi's arrival.

Heidi held out her teddy bear. 'He's gotta queek,' she informed Adam happily.

Adam took a large swallow of his wine. Heidi was wearing a soft pink pyjama suit which set off the shoulder-length blonde curls to perfection. Wide blue eyes were fastened trustingly on him. He could almost feel the touch of her small body as he had when he'd broken her fall at the park. Adam shoved the sensation away ruthlessly. He was keyed up quite enough with what he intended talking to Hannah about tonight. One thing at a time. Gritting his teeth, he forced a smile. Surely Hannah would be able to sense that this wasn't a good time.

'Back to bed, darling,' Hannah instructed.

Heidi advanced into the room. 'I gotta queek, too,' she confided to Adam. 'Just like teddy.'

Adam groaned inwardly. He knew Heidi had a squeak. He'd seen Hannah cuddle and tickle the little girl. Just as he had once done to Maddy. He shuffled further back in his chair but Heidi kept coming. Hannah was rising on the other side of the fireplace.

'I'll tuck you back in,' Hannah offered firmly. She held out her hand. 'Come on.'

'No. I want to be queeked.'

'I'll queek you.' Hannah was sounding flustered now.

'No,' Heidi stated. She moved faster towards Adam. 'Him!'

'No.' Adam tried to add weight to Hannah's authority. Small pink arms attached themselves to his leg. It was too much. Adam stood up hurriedly. Heidi lost her grip and tumbled backwards, knocking her head on the tiled hearth. Adam heard Hannah gasp with horror. He also saw the look of hurt bewilderment on Heidi's face in the split second before it crumpled into a mixture of outrage and anguish.

Hannah had seen the look as well. She gathered Heidi into her arms with the speed of a hunting lioness and rounded on Adam in a fury.

'How *dare* you push my child?'

'I didn't push her,' Adam contradicted calmly. 'It was an accident.' He reached out to touch the bump he could see on Heidi's forehead.

Hannah swivelled, wrenching Heidi out of reach. 'Don't touch her,' she snarled.

'For God's sake, Hannah.' Adam was suddenly just as angry. He had to raise his voice over Heidi's shrieks. 'I wasn't trying to *hurt* her.'

'Well, you managed without trying, then,' Hannah said scathingly.

'It's only a bump.' Adam couldn't help his disparaging tone. He was angry at his own loss of control. The self-protection he'd unconsciously tried to resurrect had back fired disastrously, and now Hannah was overreacting to the point of being ridiculous.

'I'm not talking about her physical injury,' Hannah said icily. She rocked Heidi in her arms and the child's sobs receded. 'You rejected her. You might as well have pushed her deliberately.'

'For God's sake, Hannah,' Adam said again.

Heidi gave a loud hiccup and then stuck her thumb into her mouth, turning to give Adam an accusing glare as though backing up her mother's standpoint.

Adam shook his head wearily. 'We don't need this.'

'No,' Hannah agreed coldly. 'We don't. Why don't you just go, Adam? Leave us alone.'

Adam could swear a chill breeze gusted from nowhere and then died, to create the icy stillness that followed Hannah's suggestion.

'Is that what you want me to do, Hannah?'

'Nobody is going to hurt my child, Adam.' Hannah sounded calm now. Decisive. 'Physically or emotionally.'

'It's not what you—'

'Just go,' Hannah interrupted. 'Get out, Adam. Get out of my life.' Hannah cradled her daughter more closely. 'Get out of *our* lives.'

CHAPTER EIGHT

THINGS could have been worse.

A lot worse. If Adam had actually followed through with his intention of baring his soul, painfully peeling away the remnants of that damaged shell, then there would have been no hope of ever rebuilding it. The materials and strength required were simply too hard to find. As it was, the repair job was major but not impossible. Adam had spent most of the night answering the challenge and he was bone weary when he arrived at headquarters the following morning to start his second day shift.

Adam could handle the exhaustion. In a way he welcomed the distance from reality that it imparted. His patients wouldn't notice any decrease in the level of professional concern and skill he would deliver, but Adam didn't give a damn about himself. Or about Hannah. He hadn't needed her forceful directive. He was out of her life. For good this time.

Responding to the ringing telephone as he walked past was just as automatic as everything else probably would be today.

'Duty room,' Adam informed the caller.

'Could I speak to Ivan Moresby, please?'

Adam glanced at the wall clock. It was 6.30 a.m. 'He's not here yet.' Adam was frowning as he tried to place the vaguely familiar voice. 'You could try again in ten minutes. Or would you like me to take a message?'

'It's Norma Duncan speaking. Hannah's mother.'

Of course. The internal alarm signal didn't even get a

132

chance to sound before Adam ruthlessly killed the switch. 'Adam Lewis, here, Norma. What's the problem?'

'Hannah won't be coming in to work today.'

'Oh?' Adam pushed his fingers through his hair. Relief and concern began a minor struggle. He mentally extracted the relief and held onto it. 'Why is that, Norma?'

'I don't think she's over this bug she's had,' Norma told him. 'She looked absolutely awful when I came home last night and I don't think she slept at all.'

Adam listened dispassionately. She'd get over it. It had been her choice after all. If she hadn't turned on him so aggressively they might have had a chance to talk. *He* might have had—and taken—the opportunity to explain his over-reaction to Heidi's advances. Not a ghost of a chance of that happening now. No way.

Norma was still speaking. 'And then when I made her a cup of tea this morning, she started vomiting. There's no way she's up to working.'

'Of course not,' Adam agreed readily. 'Make sure she has a good rest. If she goes any length of time with not being able to keep fluids down I would suggest you call a doctor.'

'I'll do that anyway,' Norma responded. 'I'll get Gerry Prescott to call in later this morning.'

'And I'll let Ivan Moresby know as soon as he comes in. We'll arrange cover for the next two nights as well. I think Hannah should really take enough time to make sure she's well.'

'Oh, I don't think she'd be too happy about that. She'll probably be fine by tomorrow. She's worried about getting all the hours of road time she needs before this course that's coming up.'

'That won't be a problem,' Adam assured Norma. 'And I'm sure Ivan will say the same thing. Tell Hannah we don't want to see her here before next week. She needs to make quite sure she's completely over things.' Adam would be able to ensure the roster for partners on Blue shift was adjusted if necessary by then. The timing was ideal. Hannah wasn't the only one who might need the space of more than a week to get over things.

Adam must have had something to do with the rostering. Hannah was on fourth call for the first time, partnered with a Grade 2 ambulance officer called Roger Marks. Roger had been off work for more than two months, recovering from a back problem, so Hannah hadn't met him before. She had, however, heard about him.

'You'll have to do all the lifting.' His first words to Hannah were hardly friendly. 'I've got to look after my back.' His gaze flicked over her. 'You're new, aren't you?'

'I've been on the road for nearly three months now,' Hannah responded.

Roger sniffed. 'Green as grass, then.' He turned away. 'I hope you're stronger than you look.'

Hannah checked the expiry dates on the ampoules of salbutamol she was holding. She didn't feel very strong at all. In fact, it seemed to have taken too much of her available strength to even arrive at work today. The time off sick hadn't helped at all. In retrospect, it would have been preferable to have forced herself to face Adam the very next day—like conquering the fear of falling by getting straight back onto a horse. Now Hannah had had a week to start having doubts. The fury had abated to allow the start of an emotional tug of war between her feelings for Adam and the bond she had with her child to gather momentum. Not that she would allow Adam any ground.

She couldn't afford to now and Hannah was aware of a numbing sensation of disappointment enveloping her life.

It was grief rather than disappointment, really. Adam's total rejection of her daughter had killed what might have been far more swiftly and finally than anything else could have done. Hannah slotted the ampoules of salbutamol back into the resuscitation kit with a sigh and eyed the supplies of IV equipment. Not that they would be used today. Roger Marks wasn't qualified to give IV therapy, and if they were sent to any seriously unwell patients they would have to call for backup. Now in his late forties, Hannah's partner for the day had never been particularly enamoured of his career from what Hannah had learned. She could also understand how his nickname of 'Groucho' had originated.

Perhaps it was all for the best. Hannah snapped the latches shut on the kit. She had come back to work today determined not to let her disastrous relationship with Adam undermine the satisfaction this job was capable of providing. To walk away from both Adam and her much-desired career as an ambulance officer was too much of a loss to contemplate. Hannah had to hang onto her original goal and if she could do that while working with 'Groucho' Marks then she could be confident that Adam wasn't going to destroy too much of her new life.

The patients appeared to be conspiring with Roger to make Hannah's day as miserable as possible. The first call was a transfer from a hospital ward to a rest home. Hannah was sent to fetch the patient on her own. Roger had an urgent errand which Hannah suspected involved the orderly's lodge and a pot of coffee.

The patient wasn't pleased to see Hannah. 'About time,' she said acidly. 'I've been ready for over an hour.'

'I'm sorry about that, Mrs Campbell.' Hannah tried to smile pleasantly. 'Are these bags all yours?'

'Of course they are.' The elderly woman glared at Hannah. 'And make sure you don't steal anything.'

Hannah raised the back of the stretcher, positioned a pillow and unfolded a cotton blanket to cover the mattress. 'Do you think you can get out of your chair and onto the stretcher if I help you?'

'No. My leg hurts. I've already asked the nurse for a pill and they won't give it to me. Somebody's stolen my pills.'

'Oh.' If Hannah had been partnered with someone like Tom or Matt they would have exchanged a meaningful glance at this stage. They could have found some shared amusement in the situation and probably enjoyed dealing with it. As it was, Hannah had to interrupt the busy nursing staff to find some assistance to transfer her patient to the stretcher.

'She's a cantankerous old bat,' the nurse whispered to Hannah as they returned to Mrs Campbell's room. 'We're not sorry to see her go.'

'Does she need any medication for her leg?'

'She's had it. Not that she really needs anything. She came in to have an ulcer on her varicose vein treated, that's all.' The nurse winked at Hannah. 'If you ask me, the staff at the rest home were probably desperate for a few days' break.'

The staff were too busy to spare someone to help Hannah carry Mrs Campbell's luggage. The larger suitcase fitted under the stretcher but Hannah had to juggle two smaller bags and a bunch of flowers at the same time as pushing the stretcher. Progress was slow and punctuated by frequent complaints from her patient. Arriving at the ambulance bay, Hannah looked hopefully for assistance. Roger was nowhere in sight.

'Well!' Mrs Campbell sniffed. 'If you think I enjoyed that little tour around the hospital then you're gravely mistaken.'

Roger appeared finally and took the lighter end of the stretcher to load their patient.

'That girl has stolen my pills, driver,' Mrs Campbell informed him. 'And my leg hurts.'

Mrs Campbell's leg hurt all the way to the rest home. She was also cold, then too hot, then cold again. Her flowers were wilting, her spectacles were missing—undoubtedly stolen—and Roger was deliberately driving over every bump he could find on the road. On a job satisfaction scale of one to ten, the transfer didn't even rate a positive number.

The next two jobs were also transfers. When she wasn't sitting in the back with a patient, Hannah was sitting in the front with Roger, hearing about the deplorable driving habits of the elderly, all females, and anyone driving a courier van, taxi or bus. Hannah's spirits rose a little when they received a priority-three call to a private address, but a doctor had already been and Roger had no desire to waste time by repeating any assessment. Just another transfer, except that this time the patient was genuinely unwell. The middle-aged woman vomited repeatedly and managed to tip one of the containers over onto the floor. Hannah felt thoroughly unwell herself by the time they arrived at the hospital.

'I'll do the hand-over,' Roger said quickly. 'You get the truck cleaned up.'

Returning to headquarters for a late lunch-break, Hannah wasn't surprised to find she wasn't remotely hungry. She headed for the library. Maybe a textbook or two could remind her what it was that had appealed so much about this career of hers. Curled up in a chair, Hannah found she hadn't even opened the book when her pager woke her over an hour later. She read the message. Another transfer.

Blinking wearily, Hannah made her way through the staffroom to the garage. Tom and Derek were sitting at the table.

'Must have been a rotten bug,' Tom greeted Hannah. 'You don't look too good.'

'I'm fine, thanks.' Hannah managed a smile. More pagers sounded and the men rose to follow Hannah.

'Priority one.' Derek was reading his pager. 'Chest pain.'

'Not another one!' Tom held the door open for Hannah then moved swiftly past. The beacons on their ambulance were already flashing as Hannah crossed the garage floor. She ignored the incoming ambulance. She knew who would be driving Unit 641. Opening the passenger door of her own vehicle, Hannah found Roger glaring at her.

'You'll have to get a bit quicker than that,' he admonished. 'You're not being paid to sleep on the job, you know.'

Even sleeping off the job proved difficult for Hannah that night. She kissed her daughter goodbye the following morning and wondered why she was leaving home at all. Norma looked worried.

'Are you still sure you want to keep this up?'

'That's what I need to find out, Mum. It would be a bit pathetic if I let a broken romance put me off a career I've wanted for so long.'

'Adam Lewis is a fool,' Norma stated with conviction. 'And I've a good mind to tell him what I think of the way he's treated you.'

'It's over, Mum,' Hannah sighed. 'I've just got to get over it and get on with my job.'

Norma's smile was encouraging. 'Let's hope today's an improvement on yesterday.'

Hannah gave a half-hearted grin. 'Couldn't be much worse. I guess things can only improve.'

Despite being rostered on with Roger again, the day did seem to get off to a better start with a priority-one call to a man seen staggering along the side of a main road. When they arrived at the scene, they found a young man now sitting on a traffic island.

'He could hardly walk,' a witness told them excitedly. 'He was shouting and swearing at the cars and he fell over almost in front of one.'

'He's drunk,' Roger decided.

Hannah wasn't so sure. She couldn't smell any alcohol and the man seemed too well dressed and clean to have been out on the town all night.

'What's your name, sir?'

The man pushed her away. 'Get lost!' His speech was slurred.

Hannah turned to the witness. 'Did he hit his head when he fell? Was he unconscious at all?'

'Come on, let's get him in the truck.' Roger took hold of the man's arm and pulled him to his feet. 'We're blocking traffic.'

'He might have a head injury.' Hannah took the man's other arm to help him up the back steps and onto a stretcher.

'Can't see any.' Roger put his hand firmly on the man's shoulder when he tried to get up. 'Stay where you are,' he ordered.

The man slumped back, mumbling incoherently. Roger was already climbing back into the driver's seat. Hannah unwound a blood-pressure cuff but the patient pushed her away roughly as soon as she touched his arm.

'Get off,' he shouted. 'Leave me alone.'

'What's your name?' Hannah tried to establish contact again. 'Do you know where you are?'

The only answer she received was a loud snore. Hannah picked up a penlight torch. This time she wasn't pushed away as she lifted the man's eyelids to check his pupils. They were equal and reactive but Hannah was concerned by the dropping level of consciousness. She felt his head but could find no evidence of injury. Feeling for a pulse, she noted the clammy skin and shook the man's shoulder.

'Can you hear me, sir?' she called. 'Open your eyes.' She got no response. Hannah was now seriously worried. 'Roger? The GCS is dropping. I think we'd better call for some backup.'

'We're only ten minutes away from the hospital.' Roger sounded annoyed.

Hannah was balancing herself against the stretcher as she hooked up an oxygen mask. 'Pull over, please,' she ordered. 'I'm not happy with this patient's condition.'

She could hear Roger resignedly radioing for backup as he slowed. The thought that Adam could arrive at any minute didn't bother Hannah. She hoped it would be him. They needed help.

'He's lost his swallow reflex,' she informed Roger. 'And he's got a tachycardia.'

'Use some suction,' Roger directed. 'And get an oral airway in. I'll put the monitor on.'

Hannah was relieved to see Roger responding under the pressure but she still wasn't happy. 'He's really clammy,' she pointed out. 'Should we do a blood glucose?'

Roger was fumbling with the ECG electrodes. 'In a minute.'

Hannah lifted the oxygen mask and used the suction tube to clear fluid from the man's mouth. She could hear the wail of an approaching siren. The back door of the ambulance was pulled open as she was measuring for the size of airway required.

Adam's presence was instantly reassuring. 'What's the history?'

'Seen staggering and abusing traffic,' Roger told him. 'Appeared intoxicated according to a witness.'

'What's the blood-glucose level?'

'We're just getting around to that.' Roger had the small kit in his hand. Adam took it and handed it to his partner, Matt. 'I'll get a line in,' he said tersely.

Hannah would have liked to have assisted Adam with the supplies for getting an IV line established, but she was trapped at the head end of the stretcher. With three men and an open paramedic kit on the floor there was simply no room to move. Adam looked at her only briefly.

'Change that mask to a non-rebreather and give him fifteen litres a minute.'

Hannah changed the mask and the oxygen flow. Adam had the IV line in place now. She reached into the cupboard above her head to find a bag of saline and a giving set, but when she turned back she found Adam had taken the same supplies from his own kit. He didn't need her help.

'Blood glucose is 2 mmol,' Matt reported. The level was far too low. Their patient was in a hypoglycaemic crisis.

'Draw up some glucose,' Adam directed. He took the end of the giving set he had attached to the bag of saline and plugged it onto the line in the man's hand. Opening the flow to a fast drip, Adam took the large syringe from Matt. 'I'll do this,' he announced. 'Let's get moving.

Matt, you follow with our truck.' Adam glanced at Hannah again as they moved away. 'What was his GCS when you found him?'

'About fourteen,' Hannah responded. 'But it dropped rapidly.'

'Did it not occur to you to check his blood-glucose level?'

'He wasn't very co-operative to begin with.'

'And could you smell any alcohol?'

'No.' Hannah bit her lip. 'And there was so sign of any head injury.'

'It takes thirty seconds to do a blood glucose.' Adam sounded weary. 'Maybe you'll remember next time that it's one of the most important tests to do with a patient who has an altered level of consciousness. Even if they *have* been drinking, the symptoms might be masking a far more serious condition.' Adam looked up at the monitor. The erratic trace had settled into a more normal pattern. 'The least you could have done was have some basic monitoring in place. You're lucky you didn't end up with an arrest to deal with.'

Hannah didn't need Adam to spell out how disappointed he was in her performance. His tone of voice said quite enough. The fact that Roger hadn't done his job as senior officer adequately was no excuse. Hannah would be trying a lot harder from now on. She would also be happy if their only calls for the rest of the day were routine transfers. That way they were unlikely to need any paramedic backup and Adam could keep his disappointment to himself.

Hannah was crewed with Matt for the next two nights. She did her best to make her avoidance of Adam as subtle as possible, both at the hospital and headquarters, but Matt obviously knew what was going on.

'I know it's none of my business,' Matt told Hannah quietly during a period of downtime, 'but he's my best mate and I don't like to see him so unhappy.' Matt grinned half-heartedly. 'He's been hell to work with for the last few days.'

'He'll get over it.' Hannah pretended that the television documentary they had been watching was still fascinating her. 'There was no future for us, Matt. It should never have even started.'

Matt grunted, clearly unconvinced. He glanced at Hannah's stern profile and sighed with resignation. 'I guess you're right,' he muttered. 'He'll get over it.'

Of course he would. And so would Hannah...eventually. After four days off it became a little easier to convince herself that things might somehow work themselves out. Roger was absent again with a sore back the following week and Hannah found herself partnered with Tom. She was happy to spend time discussing children. Hannah found she was missing Heidi badly during her working hours at the moment. Maybe the sacrifice she was making to take up this career wasn't worth it after all and giving up the job would be the answer to all her problems.

The call that week to go to Ivan's office was faintly alarming. What had she done wrong? The only thing Hannah could think of was that Adam had finally made a complaint about her management of that hypoglycaemic patient. She had made a point of following the case up, however, and had discovered later the same day that the hypoglycaemia had been reversed effectively and that the patient had regained consciousness shortly after arrival in the emergency department. He had been discharged that evening. Maybe it took this long for a formal complaint to be attended to. Hannah entered the station manager's office with trepidation, sitting quickly at Ivan's invitation.

'I'm worried about you, Hannah.' Ivan settled his glasses more firmly onto the bridge of his nose. 'You made such a good start on the job. All the reports I had about you were positive to say the least. You've been here, what, three months now?'

Hannah nodded. Her hands twisted themselves together in her lap. Adam *had* said something. 'Has someone made a complaint about me?'

'Good heavens, no. That's not why I asked you to come and see me.' Ivan frowned and his glasses slipped forward again. 'You just don't seem very happy. Are you finding the job isn't what you expected it to be?'

'I didn't really know what to expect.' Hannah was relieved to find she wasn't in some kind of trouble. 'I still don't. Every call is different. It's one of the things I love about the job.'

'Hmm.' Ivan was staring at her thoughtfully. 'I'm not the only one who's concerned about you, Hannah. You're very quiet and nobody sees you even when you're on station.'

'I'm usually in the library.' Hannah knew that people would eventually comment on her avoidance of the staff-room. Ivan probably knew the reason as well as everybody else did by now. She could imagine that the station manager wouldn't approve of relationships between staff members leading to acrimony on shifts. 'I've got the Grade 1 course and exams coming up next week,' she added. 'I thought I'd just get a bit of extra study in.'

'Very commendable.' Ivan nodded but Hannah could tell that he didn't entirely accept her explanation. He cleared his throat. 'We all respond to stress in different ways, Hannah. This job can be very hard on a personal level. The type of work we do inevitably takes a toll on our emotional strength. That can have a flow-on effect to our relationships both at home and on the job.'

Hannah fingered the end of her braid. Was Ivan planning some sort of counselling session with the aim of getting her and Adam back together again? If so, she had better disillusion him before it went any further.

'My relationships are exactly the way I want them,' she said clearly. 'I know I might have seemed a bit antisocial lately but, as I said, I've been taking advantage of the library. I've got a young daughter at home. It's harder to find the time to study.'

Ivan nodded again but then sighed. 'I'm not trying to pry into your personal life, Hannah. It just struck me that things haven't been the same since that incident I attended with you a couple of weeks ago. Where that young mother died in the car fire.' He looked at Hannah over the top of this glasses. 'You didn't come to the debriefing. It was your first major incident. I thought it might have a bearing on your state of mind, that's all. I wanted to make sure you realised that one of my functions is to be available if you ever need someone to talk to.'

'Oh.' Hannah's defensiveness faded in the face of Ivan's concern. 'Thank you.'

'It was a distressing case. For everybody involved.'

'Yes.' Hannah looked away. It had been the blackest day Hannah had known since the day Ben had died. First the horrific death of the woman and then the death of her relationship with Adam. No wonder people had noticed she was less than happy. 'I guess it has made me reconsider things a little,' she admitted.

'And has it changed your mind about wanting to be an ambulance officer?'

'I don't think so.' Hannah kept her gaze down. Her doubts about this career had nothing to do with any particular case. 'I think I'm quite capable of handling the stress that comes from that kind of incident.'

'I hope so. It would be a loss to the service if you decided you couldn't.' There was a short silence. 'Would you like to consider a change of shift?' Ivan asked unexpectedly.

Hannah's gaze flicked up. 'Why do you ask?'

'There's a lot of people you probably don't know very well,' Tom said casually. 'Red shift covers your days off, for instance, so you never see them. It looks like Eddie is going to be away for a while yet. His leg is taking its time healing. We could easily put the overtime cover onto Blue shift instead.'

And Hannah would never have to work with Adam. Even as backup. She might not see him for weeks at a time. She wouldn't have to consider leaving her job. She should jump at the chance. It would make life a lot easier. Hannah could get over the pervasive misery that had surrounded her for the last two weeks. If she didn't see Adam maybe she could forget his smile and that intent way of listening and that habit of ruffling his hair with his fingers. She might even be able to forget why she had fallen in love with the man. Common sense told her that distance was the only answer. Was she such a masochist that she still wanted to work nearby?

'Think about it.' Ivan gave up on waiting for her response. 'You've got two weeks in the classroom coming up. Let me know after that.'

It was like old times. The induction group were gathered in the same classroom. Only now their number was greatly reduced and Hannah was the only woman present.

They all wore uniforms now as well and they were all a little older and wiser after the months of intensive road time. Hannah had seen Derek every day at work but the changes in the other men surprised her.

Michael had lost his over-confident air. He was quieter now and as keen to hear others talk as to speak himself. He and Ross had both been working in one of the outlying city stations.

'It's a great team,' Ross told Hannah. 'Our instructor for this course, Jim Melton, is one of our paramedics.'

Hannah glanced at Michael. Wasn't Jim the one Michael had had the argument with over a patient's treatment?

'He really knows what he's talking about,' Michael added. 'We should learn a lot.'

'I wish Adam was taking the course.' Eddie had propped his crutches beside his desk. 'Not that I'm going to pass,' he added wistfully. 'At least, not until I make up my road time.'

'You'll get there,' Hannah said kindly. 'How's your leg doing?'

'Improving. I'm having physio every day.' Eddie's smile at Hannah was surprisingly apologetic. She was puzzled until Ross grinned at Eddie.

'What's this I hear about you and that blonde physiotherapist?'

Eddie blushed and Hannah smiled. His allegiance had been transferred and Hannah was pleased for him. And for herself. There was no point in any man, other than Adam, expressing interest in her and she couldn't have summoned the reserves needed to cushion Eddie's ego if he had tried again. She sat down with a relieved sigh that caught John's attention.

'You look like you've lost weight,' he told Hannah. 'Have you been working too hard?'

'I got a bug from a patient a while back,' Hannah explained. 'It was a bit hard to shake off.' She smiled at John. 'You, however, look fitter than ever.'

'I'm in training. I'm taking leave after this course to go and do an Ironman event in Hawaii.'

'Are you? They don't mind?'

'I'm not giving them a choice.' John shrugged. 'My competitions are as much a priority as this job.' He sat down beside Hannah. 'To tell you the truth, the novelty has worn off just a bit. I get pretty sick of doing transfer work. It's enough to make me wonder whether I want to stay in the job.'

Hannah nodded. Maybe the novelty was wearing off for her as well, but she still knew she didn't want to give up her career choice.

Michael was also nodding as he arranged pens and paper on his desk. 'But then you get a real job and you remember why we're here.'

Hannah searched for her own pen. She needed to remember that as well. She hadn't even met Adam before she'd joined the service so he shouldn't be the main reason she still wanted to stay.

'I wouldn't want to be doing anything else,' Ross agreed. 'I'm even ready for some heavy-duty swotting for this exam.'

The academic work over the next two weeks was to be intensive. It was divided into medical conditions for the first week and trauma for the second. Hannah found the workload demanding as they began by covering the cardiovascular and respiratory systems from their anatomy to the types of conditions they could present with and the appropriate emergency treatment. Hannah's notes during class time were copious. Her referral to textbooks at home was time-consuming. She used any left over time to swot for the exams.

'Test me, Mum,' she directed Norma, long after Heidi was tucked up in her bed and sound asleep.

Norma reluctantly accepted the pile of flash cards Hannah had made.

'OK. What are the three pathological processes that produce airway obstruction leading to an acute asthmatic attack?'

Hannah shut her eyes. 'Bronchospasm, which causes widespread reversible narrowing of the airways. Swelling of the mucous membranes of the bronchial walls and plugging of the bronchi by secretions.'

Norma nodded as Hannah opened her eyes. She selected another card. 'What diseases other than asthma may produce wheezing?'

'Left heart failure,' Hannah responded promptly. 'Also foreign body aspiration, toxic fume inhalation, pulmonary embolism, allergic reactions and…and…' She bit her lip. 'I've missed something.'

'Chronic bronchitis,' Norma supplied.

'Damn! I knew that,' Hannah groaned. 'Ask me another one.'

'It's time to stop, love. It's nearly midnight.'

'Just one more,' Hannah begged.

'This is the last one,' Norma said firmly. She glanced at a card. 'What the signs and symptoms of left heart failure?'

'Restlessness and confusion,' Hannah began promptly. 'Difficulty breathing, fast breathing. Um…raised blood pressure and…' Hannah buried her face in her hands. 'God, I can't remember. I wish I wasn't so tired.'

'You need some sleep,' Norma said with concern.

'You're overdoing this and you're not eating properly. It's no wonder you're so tired all the time.' She looked at Hannah and shook her head. 'You know, I still don't think you're completely over that bug you had.'

'That was weeks ago.'

'Yes, but you were vomiting on and off for days and you've never looked quite well since. I want you to go and see Dr Prescott.'

Hannah sighed. 'I'll be fine, Mum.'

'Tomorrow.' Norma's tone wasn't inviting any argument. 'I'll be making an appointment for you at 5.30 p.m. You should have finished your class by then. All right?'

'If it'll keep you happy,' Hannah said with resignation. 'I'll go and see him. He'll only say there's nothing wrong with me. I'll be wasting his time.'

'Let him be the judge of that,' Norma advised.

Gerry Prescott didn't seem to think Hannah was wasting his time at all but, then, he was a very nice man. Hannah made no objections to any of the questions or tests the older doctor wished to include in his thorough check-up of her.

'Of course, I'm only doing this to keep Mum happy,' Hannah warned him.

'She is worried about you,' Dr Prescott agreed.

'I'm fine, really.' Hannah had finished dressing again. She appeared from behind the curtain and sat down beside Dr Prescott's desk. 'I'm just a bit run down, I expect, from coping with a new job and everything.'

'Are your periods usually regular?' Gerry Prescott asked casually.

'Usually.'

'When was the last one?'

Hannah's brow creased. 'I can't remember,' she confessed.

'Would it have been more than two months ago?'

'Oh, no,' Hannah said confidently. 'I'm never that late. It must have been about...' Her voice trailed off as she met Dr Prescott's calm gaze. 'You can't mean...'

Dr Prescott nodded slowly. 'You're definitely pregnant, Hannah. About six to eight weeks, I'd say. We'll book you in for a scan if you like so we can confirm dates.'

'That's simply not possible.' Hannah shook her head.

'Didn't your mother tell me you were in a relationship fairly recently?'

'Yes, but we took precautions,' Hannah insisted. 'We were very careful. I can't be pregnant.'

'Nothing's infallible, I'm afraid.' Dr Prescott was watching Hannah with concern. 'I can see this is a shock for you, my dear, but there's absolutely no doubt. Both the urine test and the physical exam were positive.'

'But I *can't* be pregnant,' Hannah whispered. The awful repercussions the news might produce were beginning to crowd her mind. 'I just *can't* be.'

CHAPTER NINE

'YOU can't be pregnant.' Adam's face could have been carved from stone judging by his lack of expression. 'We were careful. We took precautions.'

'I know.' Hannah had turned away. She was looking out the window of Adam's living room. 'Unfortunately, nothing's infallible. I've had the tests, including an ultrasound scan. I'm eight weeks pregnant.'

'So it's not too late, then.'

'Too late?' Hannah swung back, having only just caught the muttered words. Her voice rose sharply. 'Too late for what, Adam?'

Now Adam was avoiding her gaze. He sat, hunched, at one end of his dining table, one hand shielding his eyes. A half-eaten meal lay pushed to the centre of the table, abandoned when Hannah had called unannounced.

'Too late for us?' Hannah suggested coldly. Her breath was expelled in an incredulous huff. 'It's always been too late for us, Adam.'

'That wasn't what I meant,' Adam ground out.

'Oh.' Hannah's tone was heavily understanding. 'You'd rather I'd just made the problem disappear, is that it?' Hannah was becoming angered by Adam's lack of eye contact. It was like talking to someone through a wall. 'Maybe *I* should just disappear,' Hannah snapped. 'Resign from my job and remove myself entirely from your life. Would you like that, Adam?' Hannah folded her arms around herself. 'Don't worry, it will probably happen. I won't be able to keep the job if I'm pregnant.' She was still staring at Adam's profile. 'And even if I wasn't I'm not sure I want to work anywhere near you.' Even in the future. Even if she had the baby and accepted her mother's enormously generous offer to help her care for two children.

'Damn it, Hannah!' Adam's fist came down, thumping the table so hard the cutlery bounced on the abandoned plate, making Hannah flinch. 'I didn't expect this to happen. I did my best to make bloody sure it *wouldn't* happen.' He pushed himself to his feet. 'I told you right from the start that my future doesn't include children. Mine or anyone else's. *Especially* not mine.'

The look Hannah was receiving was worse than the anguished thump on the table. The pain beneath the accusing glare made Hannah realise just how deeply Adam felt about the issue. How could she have even entertained the idea that he could accept her daughter? Let alone that the revelation of this pregnancy could somehow alter his stance.

Hannah's anger fled. She was frightened by the depth of emotion she could see shimmering beneath Adam's features. She couldn't believe that she was the sole cause, but whatever private hell she had unleashed was obviously more than Adam could handle easily. If she pushed just a little harder she might find out the truth, but Hannah felt too emotionally vulnerable herself right now to take anyone else's anguish on board. Even Adam's.

'I shouldn't have come,' she said calmly. She tore her gaze away from Adam to give him a chance to collect himself. 'I thought you had the right to know.'

The long silence was charged with things left unsaid. Hannah stared out of the window again at the fading daylight. It was Adam's turn to speak. It was his choice in which direction he took them now. When he did speak, his voice was raw.

'I do love you, Hannah.'

Hannah said nothing. The words hurt more than any anger could have done because she knew what was coming next.

'I'm just not prepared—not capable—of handling *this*.'

Hannah turned slowly. 'What do you want me to do, Adam?'

He almost shrugged. 'It's your body,' he said tonelessly. 'So I guess it's your choice.' He looked away. 'It's not the first time you've been faced with the prospect of raising a child without a father.'

Hannah gasped. 'How could you even make a comparison? I had no choice but to go on without Heidi's father.'

'There's always a choice, Hannah.'

The colour drained from Hannah's face. She could feel it leaving, accompanied by a faint wave of a now familiar nausea. 'I loved Ben.' The words trembled only slightly. 'And I wanted my baby. *Our* baby.'

'And this one?'

Hannah pressed her lips together tightly. She wasn't going to tell Adam that her feelings for him had been far deeper than any she had ever felt for any man—even Ben. Or that, even now, despite the obstacle that Adam's aversion to children had provided, she didn't want to contemplate a future without him. Adam's rejection of Heidi had more than hinted at how difficult it could prove to overcome the obstacle but Hannah still hadn't been able to let him go. The pull from opposite directions, with Adam on one side and Heidi on the other, had been enough to make the last few weeks unbearably unhappy.

Hannah couldn't take any more. Right now she wasn't even sure whether any part of her feelings towards Adam were still intact. If they were, she wasn't going to add to this emotional storm they were both desperately trying to weather.

'As you said, Adam. It's my choice.' Hannah made her feet move. She headed towards the door.

'I expect you'll manage—whatever you decide.' Adam was following her.

'I expect I will,' Hannah said tightly. 'As you pointed out, I've had some practice with fatherless children. I can manage one. Maybe another one won't make too much of a difference.'

'If I can help with anything…financial, let me know.' Adam sounded uncomfortable. 'I've heard that the clinic in Cambridge Terrace offers the best maternity care in the city. I've also heard that it's rather expensive.'

Hannah stepped outside. The Cambridge Clinic was well known for its excellent facilities and care. It was also known to provide discreet terminations and Hannah had no intention of even considering that option.

'I expect I'll manage, thank you.' Hannah couldn't quite meet Adam's eyes before turning away. 'Goodbye, Adam.'

'Hannah?'

The soft call came when she was halfway to the gate. Hannah ignored the appeal. Right now there was nothing more that could be said. They were both suffering enough. She shook her head and latched the gate firmly shut behind her.

Adam slammed the gate shut as he headed to work the next morning. He was so wound up he barely registered the route into headquarters. The dilemma Hannah had presented him with last night couldn't be banished from his thoughts for an instant. He was facing a hell of a day.

The only consolation was that Hannah was confined to a classroom so there would be no chance of any further discussion until after 6 p.m.

There would *be* further discussion, however. The totally unsatisfactory ending to the meeting last night had eaten at Adam. He had almost rung Hannah at 4 a.m.

Don't do it, he'd wanted to say. Please, don't do it.

How could he have even allowed the notion of ending the pregnancy to be aired? It was unthinkable. A cold and callous solution to what shouldn't even be a problem. He and Hannah loved each other. Or had done. Could an emotion that powerful be destroyed by the turmoil they had put themselves through over the last three months?

The turmoil *he* had put them through, Adam amended grimly. Hannah had done nothing other than offer him her love and try and protect her daughter. Did she still have any feelings left for him now? She hadn't said so yesterday. She had spoken of her love for Heidi's father and the desire to keep that baby, but she had said nothing about him or how she felt about his child. She'd said it was her choice and that she would manage. And Adam had let her go.

Parking his Jeep, Adam tried to clear his head as he marched towards the garage. This was work. Even through the best and worst times his relationship with Hannah had provided so far, Adam had managed to keep his personal and professional agendas separate. Today was going to test that ability to the limit. Thank goodness he was crewing with Matt. A day with Tom and his tendency to discuss his baby at every opportunity would have been intolerable. The only thing worse would be a call to a maternity emergency.

Precisely such a call came in just before 4 p.m.

'Priority one,' Matt relayed to Adam as they ran towards Unit 241. 'Woman in labour—12B Gasgoine Street.'

It was a good distraction to drive so fast. It took intense concentration and nerves of steel to spot all the hazards before they became problems, to judge the spaces available and try to predict the reactions of other road users. The noise helped as well. Adam kept the siren on, flipping to a yelp at every intersection and underscoring the urgency with long blasts on the air horn. The response time for the incident was excellent—four minutes from receiving the call to knocking on the door of the Gasgoine Street property.

The door opened instantly to reveal an agitated-looking man in his early thirties. 'Thank God,' he said to Adam. 'We've got to hurry. We haven't got much time.' He handed Adam a suitcase. 'I'll just go and get Pamela.'

Adam glanced at Matt who returned his frown. They were both disturbed by the man's anxiety. Adam needed to assess the situation before they all found themselves out in the street. Putting the suitcase down, Adam strode into the house, carrying his kit. He followed the direction the man had taken and found him helping a woman to put her coat on. She was sitting on a double bed.

'This is my wife, Pamela,' the man explained, catching sight of Adam in the doorway. 'We're all ready to go.'

Adam smiled at the woman. 'Hi, Pamela. I'm Adam. Is this your first baby?'

Pamela shook her head and Adam raised his eyebrows. First-time nerves might have explained the edge of panic he could sense in the couple.

'How far are you on in the pregnancy?'

'Thirty-six weeks.'

'And you've been having some contractions?'

Pamela's husband took hold of her elbow. He helped

her to stand up. 'We haven't got time for all these questions,' he said impatiently. 'We've got to get moving. This is an emergency.'

'I'd prefer to know what kind of emergency we're dealing with,' Adam said calmly. 'We may be more help to Pamela here than when we're on the road.'

'I feel dizzy, Bruce,' Pamela said anxiously. 'And I think I'm going to be sick.'

Matt came in and deposited the maternity pack on the floor as Adam moved to support Pamela.

'Sit down again,' he directed. 'This is my partner, Matt. Bruce, could you find Pamela a bowl, please?'

'I've got one here.' Bruce let go of his wife's arm reluctantly. 'She was sick a while back when the contractions started.'

'How far apart are these contractions?'

'Only two minutes,' Bruce informed him. 'And they're lasting at least sixty seconds. That's why we've got to get going.'

Adam was taking Pamela's pulse. He then moved his hand to her abdomen which felt rock hard. Pamela's face twisted.

'It's starting again,' she groaned. 'I think I need to push.' Seconds later she cried, 'I *am* going to be sick.'

Bruce held the bowl for his wife and Adam turned to Matt. 'We can't transport yet. It looks like an imminent delivery. We'll have to deliver here and then transport them both.'

'You can't do that!' Bruce was holding the bowl with one hand and supporting Pamela's head with the other. 'It's all arranged at the hospital. We need the intensive care unit available for the baby.'

'Are you expecting problems?' Adam caught Pamela as

she collapsed backwards onto the bed. She drew her knees up and groaned again loudly.

'It's too late, Bruce. I really *have* to push this time.'

Matt had the shears ready to cut Pamela's underwear clear. Adam folded a towel and placed it under her hips. Bruce took hold of Pamela's hand.

'It's all right, love.' He was trying hard to sound calmer. 'These guys will know what to do.'

'What problems are you expecting?' Adam asked.

'Same as last time,' Pamela gasped. The contraction had ended but Adam knew there was no chance of moving the mother safely now. He could see that the baby's head was not far off crowning. Another contraction or two and they would have a potentially sick baby on their hands.

'Which was?' he queried tersely.

'It's a connective tissue disorder. A rather rare syndrome.' Bruce spoke quietly. 'The main problem is the anatomy of the heart and lungs. The baby may well have problems starting to breathe.'

Adam needed a deep breath himself. He finished tying on the gown he had removed from the maternity pack. Matt had brought in some more equipment. He positioned the suction unit next to Pamela in case she vomited again. Then he hooked up an oxygen mask to the portable cylinder. Adam put on the lightweight plastic goggles and donned surgical gloves. The parents' extreme anxiety was now perfectly comprehensible.

'Did you lose your first baby at birth?' he asked gently.

'No.' It was Pamela who spoke. 'Bethany lived for six months. It was longer than we'd been allowed to hope for. And she was able to be at home. She was such a happy wee thing.'

Adam was taken aback. Surely it was still a major loss.

Even worse at six months than it would have been at birth before they'd had a chance to bond with the baby.

'And you know that this baby is suffering from the same condition?'

'Oh, yes.' Bruce nodded. 'They didn't think it would happen a second time but we found out when Pamela had the second scan at about twelve weeks.'

Adam was astonished. How could the parents have carried on, knowing that they would be facing the same trauma they had already gone through? Not only that, but they were both so anxious that this baby would survive the birth.

'It's coming!' Pamela gripped her husband's hand and raised her head from the pillow as she pushed.

Adam placed his gloved fingers on the infant's skull as it crowned, exerting gentle pressure to prevent an explosive birth. He was careful to avoid both the face and the fontanel. Feeling for the cord, Adam frowned.

'Cord's around the neck,' he told Matt quietly. 'Got some clamps?'

Matt handed Adam two clamps from the maternity supplies laid out on a towel beside him. Adam placed the clamps three inches apart and cut the cord in the space between them. He reached for the bulb syringe on the towel as the baby's head was delivered, sucking out the mouth and nose several times. The next contraction expelled the baby's body and Adam caught the slippery bundle gently, easing the legs clear and placing the baby on another clean towel. He wiped the mouth and nose with a gauze pad and suctioned them again with the syringe.

Adam concentrated on the infant. Matt was caring for Pamela who was vomiting again, crying at the same time. Bruce also had tears on his face as he stared at his baby. It didn't look good. Adam did a rapid Apgar assessment.

The baby was blue. The aid of a stethoscope let him pick up a weak heartbeat but it was less than one hundred a minute. The baby was showing no signs of expression or activity and there were only sporadic attempts at respiration. A score of three at the most.

Adam pulled the infant bag valve mask from the resuscitation kit and swiftly attached it to the oxygen supply. He ventilated carefully with just enough pressure to raise the baby's chest. It took only a tiny squeeze of the bag. After thirty seconds he checked the heart rate again. The pulse was now less than eighty beats per minutes.

Adam's face set into grim lines as he circled the baby's body with his fingers, placing both thumbs on the lower portion of the sternum. Overlapping his thumbs, he pressed just hard enough to compress the tiny chest to a depth of about half an inch. The rate was very rapid—at least one hundred and twenty compressions per minute.

Adam did the next Apgar score at five minutes. The baby was now pink with blue hands and feet. The pulse had come up to more than a hundred and the baby's face moved when it took a breath. Moving an arm, Adam found the limpness had receded.

'Some flexion,' he reported to Matt. 'I'd give it one point.'

'The respirations are improving,' Matt noted. 'But it's still slow. I'd say the total score is still only six.'

'We've doubled it.' Adam smiled for the first time since the drama had begun. He looked at the parents. 'As soon as I'm sure she's stable, we'll get you both to the hospital.'

'Placenta's arriving,' Matt commented.

'You take care of that,' Adam directed. He had turned his attention quickly back to the baby. Flicking the soles of the feet produced a weak cry, the first sound the baby had made. Pamela's pale face turned excitedly to Bruce.

'She's alive!'

Bruce sniffed loudly. 'She's beautiful,' he told Pamela.

'You'll be able to hold her in just a minute.' Adam watched as Matt finished dealing with the placenta. 'Seal that in a bag, Matt. Can you manage to get a stretcher in here on your own?'

'Sure.'

Adam was happy to note an Apgar score of nine after ten minutes. He wrapped the baby in a blanket and put her into her mother's arms. He would give them only as long as it took to tidy up the messy scene. Adam still wanted this mother and child under the care of specialists as quickly as possible.

'She looks just like Bethany,' Pamela whispered as she gazed at her newborn daughter. 'Don't you think, Bruce?'

'Peas in a pod,' Bruce agreed.

Adam rolled up soiled towels and stuffed them into a plastic bag. How could these two sound like any overjoyed new parents when they knew what they were facing? When they knew that this baby couldn't even survive for more than a few months at most. Adam knew what it was like to gaze at your own infant for the first time. How precious they were. How you couldn't help but wonder what the future held for them. What they might be like in a year's time. Or five years. Or ten. As he had done with Maddy. As he still did and would do for the rest of his life. Adam sighed as he zipped up the maternity pack case. He knew he would do the same for the child Hannah was now carrying. No matter what her decision ended up being.

'This is Bethany.' Bruce was pushing something to-

wards Adam as he loaded equipment back into his paramedic kit. 'She was three months old.'

Adam had to look at the photograph. She looked like
a normal, happy baby.

'She'd be five years old now.' Bruce smiled wistfully.
'We often wonder what she'd look like now. What it
would be like, sending her off to school.'

Adam cleared his throat. 'I know, mate,' he said gently.
'It's not easy, is it?'

Matt had prepared the stretcher. Adam cleared his
throat again.

'Let's get moving,' he suggested briskly. 'Bruce, can
you hold the baby while we help Pamela onto the
stretcher?'

Adam wanted to drive but Matt got there first. 'No way,
mate,' he told Adam sternly. 'You got to do the delivery.
Now you get to do all the paperwork as well.'

Adam managed to get most of the documentation done,
as well as monitoring both mother and baby, during the
trip to hospital. Bruce sat beside him on the spare
stretcher.

'You probably think we're mad,' Bruce said unexpectedly as they pulled into the hospital grounds. 'Choosing
to go through this again.'

Adam just smiled. It wasn't his place to express any
opinion on the matter.

'We didn't intend to get pregnant again after Bethany
but then we couldn't bring ourselves to do anything about
it. They did offer us the choice.'

'Losing Bethany was the worst thing that could have
happened to us,' Pamela added. 'But then we realised that
the few months we had with her had been the best thing
that had ever happened to us.'

'We know what to expect this time.' Bruce seemed to

want Adam to understand. 'So we'll be able to appreciate the time we do have. That's why we were so worried about getting through the birth safely.'

'We want to make the most of every minute.' Pamela cuddled her baby even closer and kissed the tip of the miniature nose. 'Every single minute.'

Adam couldn't wait until he had handed over the case to the emergency staff and the paediatric team that were awaiting their arrival. He shrugged off the congratulations on managing the difficult newborn successfully. Adam had a personal matter on his mind again. A personal emergency, in fact. He checked his watch as he climbed into the driver's seat of Unit 241 to wait for Matt. Nearly 5.15 p.m. Hannah would have finished the day in the classroom by now. She should be at home. Adam pulled out his cellphone and punched in the numbers.

The line was engaged and Adam sighed with vexation. He had to talk to Hannah. Now. It simply couldn't wait. He started the engine and released the handbrake as soon as Matt was aboard.

'What's the hurry? Have we got another call?'

'Personal errand,' Adam said curtly. 'It's urgent.'

He drove towards Hannah's house. How could he have been so mistaken all these years? To have wasted so much time being obsessed by something so negative. Pamela and Bruce had it right. Time with someone you loved was precious. Every single minute of it. The amount of pain a loss could produce only existed because of the amount of joy it had provided. He had negated the joy that Maddy had given him for years now by excluding the memories to try and avoid the pain. It was only now that he could appreciate the enormity of what he had denied himself.

Adam was already experiencing the pain of losing Hannah. He was trying to exclude those memories as well, and he hadn't even allowed himself to explore all the joyful possibilities that a relationship with Hannah could give. Possibilities that would only come if he was prepared to accept her love and trust her enough to be completely honest with her. If he was prepared to admit just how much he did want their child.

He pulled the ambulance up outside Hannah's house and ran up to the front door. He knocked, then entered. Matt looked puzzled but minded his own business. He looked more concerned, however, when Adam ran straight back out of the property he had just visited. A slightly bemused-looking older woman and a small girl stood on the verandah, watching Adam run back down the path.

Adam slammed the ambulance into motion. He flicked the switch to activate the beacons.

'What's going on?' Matt's jaw dropped. His own pager hadn't sounded. 'Where are we going?'

'The Cambridge Clinic,' Matt snapped. He turned the siren on and pressed his foot flat to the floor. 'This is a *real* emergency now.'

CHAPTER TEN

THE high wrought-iron gates stood wide open yet there was no way for the ambulance to gain access.

Adam hit the brakes and stared at the line of silent people stretched across the entrance to the Cambridge Clinic. Their linked hands created a human chain that effectively blocked the driveway.

'What the...?'

Having turned off the beacons and siren when entering Cambridge Terrace, there was now a stillness as Adam's query died into a bewildered silence.

'It's a Pro-Life protest,' Matt observed. 'Look at the placards.'

'What the hell are they doing here?'

Matt waved a hand towards the group of ultra-modern, mirror-windowed, white buildings set in manicured grounds. The Cambridge Clinic had been built as a private and exclusive obstetrics and gynaecology hospital only two years ago.

'They'll target any facility where terminations are performed.'

'But why here? And why *now*?'

'They do cater for terminations here,' Matt said reasonably. 'I thought everybody knew that.'

'For God's sake,' snapped Adam. 'Why do you think *we're* here?' He shook his head angrily. 'It's hardly the clinic's sole function. Haven't these people got a life?'

A heavy-set, middle-aged man approached the ambulance with an air of importance and tapped on the driver's window. Adam rolled it down impatiently.

'Sorry, but we can't let you through, mate.'

'Like hell you can't,' Adam growled. 'Get those people to move. This is an emergency.'

'They're all emergencies.' The man nodded sagely. 'That's why we speak for those who can't speak for themselves. We're saving lives.'

'For God's sake!' Adam raised his voice angrily. 'Move! I'm having a baby.'

'You're not!' Matt breathed incredulously. '*Are* you?'

'I bloody well hope so,' Adam muttered. 'If I'm not too late.' He bared his teeth at the protest group leader. 'If you want to save lives, mate, tell your people to get out of my way.'

Adam turned the beacons back on. He flashed the headlights. He started rolling slowly forward and gave a blast on the siren as the front bumper came within touching distance of the protesters. The line of people dropped their handholds and scattered. Adam picked up speed.

'Why today?' he ground out through gritted teeth. 'Why *now*, precisely?'

Matt was still staring, slack jawed, at his partner. 'Are you *really* having a baby?'

'No, of course not.'

'Then what are we doing here?'

'Hannah is having a baby,' Adam sighed. '*My* baby.' He slowed and then halted abruptly as he spotted the signpost. 'That is if she hasn't decided not to go through with it.'

'You mean she's considering a termination?'

'I don't know,' Adam said distractedly. He was staring at the sign. The choice of reception areas included those for the hospital, outpatient clinics, labour wards and day surgery. Antenatal classrooms, counsellors and a host of other services were also listed. 'Where would she go?' Adam muttered tensely.

'Was the problem between you two because she wants a termination?' Matt sounded puzzled. 'Doesn't she want your baby?'

'She thinks *I* don't want the baby.'

'And do you?'

'Of course I bloody do. Why do you think I'm here?' Adam drummed his fingers on the steering-wheel. 'I have to tell *her* that.'

'Could be an outpatient appointment,' Matt suggested helpfully. 'Or day surgery. Depends on how quickly they might go ahead with it. When did she make the appointment?'

'I have no idea. I only found out about the pregnancy yesterday but she said she'd already had all the tests, including a scan. She could have booked this in days ago. We'll try day surgery.' Adam decided briskly. He turned left and gunned the engine.

'What happens if we get a call, mate?'

'You'll have to go by yourself,' Adam told Matt. 'I've got to sort this out. It's an emergency.' He glanced at his watch. 'It's nearly the end of our shift, anyway.' He halted the vehicle again and wrenched the door open. 'Wait here,' he directed.

Adam took the three steps in a single bound and burst through the automatic doors as they opened. The receptionist looked startled.

'Did we call for an ambulance?' she asked in alarm.

'No. I'm looking for someone,' Adam said hurriedly. 'Hannah Duncan. Is she here?'

'Are you a relative?'

'No.' Adam's honesty was automatic. 'But it's important. I have to find her.'

'I'm afraid I can't release patient details without their
consent.' The receptionist eyed Adam's uniform again and
then looked past his shoulder to where the ambulance was
parked outside the door. She frowned anxiously. 'Are you
here in an official capacity?'

'You bet,' Adam lied with authority. 'Look, I don't
need details. I just need to know where she is.'

'Oh.' The receptionist's stern expression faltered and
she glanced towards her computer screen. 'What did you
say her name was?'

'Hannah Duncan.' Adam held his breath as the woman
tapped first one key and then another. His pager buzzed
and he ignored it.

'She's not listed as being in for day surgery.'

'Where would she be, then? Her mother told me she's
here somewhere.'

'It's a big place,' the receptionist commented unhelp-
fully. 'What has she come here *for*?'

'I don't know,' growled Adam. 'That's what I'm trying
to find out.'

'Try the main reception desk. It's the next entrance in
this block.'

Adam took the steps more slowly this time. He was
aware of his pager buzzing again as he approached the
ambulance. Matt was now sitting in the driver's seat.

'It's only a priority four,' Matt told him. 'A rest-home
transfer. I've arranged a nurse escort. I can manage and
it'll use up the rest of the shift so you're clear to stay.'

'Thanks, mate.' Adam unclipped his pager and tossed
it onto the passenger seat. 'I owe you one.'

'Just go and find Hannah,' Matt urged. 'And sort
this out.'

'Don't worry about that.' Adam nodded grimly. 'I'm not leaving until I do.'

The main reception area seemed extraordinarily busy for the late time of day. A large group of people was milling about towards one side of the large room. Adam ignored them, skirting several very pregnant women as he negotiated his way to the desk.

'Are you here for the open day, sir?' The receptionist queried brightly. 'The tour is just about to get under way.'

'No. I'm looking for someone. Hannah Duncan. I'm not sure what department she's in but she had an appointment for 5.30 p.m.'

'It's 5.40 p.m now,' the receptionist pointed out. 'Are you supposed to be with her for the appointment?'

'Yes.' Adam was getting used to being less than truthful. 'It's imperative that I'm present. I'm her husband.' Adam actually smiled. He liked the sound of that statement.

'Well, let's see.' The receptionist stepped towards her computer but was distracted by a couple who rushed up behind Adam.

'Are we too late?' the man queried anxiously.

'What for, sir?'

'The guided tour. We just read about it in the newspaper. Annie's pregnant,' the man added proudly. 'We're trying to choose the best birthing facility available.'

Adam gritted his teeth and tried to will the receptionist to hurry, but she was smiling a welcome to the newcomers.

'Congratulations. You've come to the right place, then. You're not too late. The tour's just getting under way.' The receptionist pointed to where the group of people was now leaving the reception area through a side corridor. 'If you hurry you won't miss a thing.'

'Thanks.' The man took hold of his partner's arm and they moved off quickly.

'Now, where were we?' The receptionist beamed at Adam. 'What was your wife's name again, sir?'

'Hannah,' Adam said heavily. 'Hannah Duncan.'

'That would be ''Mrs''?'

'No. Probably not.' Adam shook his head. From the corner of his eye he caught the movement of the door to the women's toilets opening. His breath came out in a huff of relief as he recognised the emerging figure. 'Never mind,' he told the receptionist. 'I've found her.'

Adam hurried past the row of comfortable armchairs. 'Hannah!'

Hannah's head swivelled and her grey eyes widened dramatically. 'Adam! What on earth are you doing here?'

'I have to talk to you.'

'It'll have to wait, Adam. I'm running late.'

Adam caught her arm. 'It can't wait. I can't let you do this, Hannah.'

'Do what?' Hannah was frowning.

'Whatever it is you came here to do.' Adam couldn't find the right words. His desperation was making him sound angry. 'I won't let you go through with it.'

'You can't stop me.' Hannah pulled her arm free. 'It's *my* choice, remember?' She walked away, taking the same direction as the tour group.

Adam's feet refused to move for a few seconds as he tried to formulate a more effective plan of action. Hannah didn't seem too keen to talk to him and who could blame her? A public place wasn't ideal to plead his case but Adam had no choice. He caught up with Hannah as she reached the back of the small crowd of sightseers.

'I want this baby,' he told her fiercely. 'Even if you don't.'

Annie was standing next to Hannah. She turned to stare open-mouthed at Adam. A woman's voice filled the silence.

'As you can see, we have perfect home-birth facilities within the safety net of a high-tech hospital setting. The king-sized bed caters for couples who wish to stay together, before, during and even after the birth.'

Annie turned away from her scrutiny of Adam to nudge her partner. 'Sounds great,' she whispered loudly.

'Hannah?' Adam muttered. 'Did you hear me?'

Hannah nodded but said nothing. She seemed to be listening as avidly as everyone else to their guide.

'The entertainment unit delivers television, video and music facilities. We encourage people to bring their favourite music in with them. The bathroom in each suite provides a full-sized spa pool.'

'This must cost a bomb,' Annie's partner muttered.

'Hannah?' Adam's voice was more than a whisper now. 'I can handle this. I can bring this baby up by myself if I need to. I've done it before.'

'What?' He had Hannah's attention now. 'What *are* you talking about, Adam?'

'Maddy,' Adam breathed on a sigh. 'My daughter.'

'You have a *daughter*?' Hannah's voice rose in astonishment. Annie's husband turned to frown at her disapprovingly.

'Had,' Adam corrected quietly. 'She died when she was two and a half.'

Hannah looked stunned. The guide's enthusiastic tone seemed incongruous.

'Let's move on towards a more traditional birth facility. I'm sure you'll also be very impressed with the theatre services we have available should they be required.'

'That's Heidi's age,' Hannah whispered.

'Of course, the consultant obstetricians and their support staff are selected for their extremely high standard of skill.' The guide was urging the group forward.

'She was very like Heidi,' Adam said. 'She even left soggy biscuits where you wouldn't want to find them. And she liked being squeaked.'

Most of the group had moved on. The guide was still standing on the chair she had used to gain enough height to speak to the large group. Now she was waiting for Adam and Hannah.

'Come along, please,' she directed. 'There's a lot to see and our time *is* limited.'

Adam and Hannah complied automatically. They walked side by side as the group filed down another corridor towards the operating theatres. The guide caught up as the progress began to slow. Wearing a tailored suit and high-heeled shoes, the woman's severe hairstyle was as businesslike as the clipboard she carried.

'I'm Miranda,' she introduced herself confidently. 'What do you think so far?'

'Ah...' Hannah appeared to have forgotten where she was. She looked around rather vaguely.

'It's fantastic,' Adam told Miranda. 'We'll probably go for that king-sized bed ourselves.'

Miranda smiled and nodded as though she would expect nothing less. She raised an arm and her voice. 'Just look through the doors and move on, please,' she called. 'Obviously we can't allow anybody inside the actual theatre. It's a sterile field.'

Hannah was standing still. 'That's how you know so much about babies,' she said suddenly. 'Why didn't you tell me before?'

'I've never told anyone,' Adam admitted. 'I've never wanted to give that much of myself to anyone.' His gaze softened and caught hold of Hannah's hands. 'Until now,' he added quietly.

Hannah's expression had changed as well. She looked almost relieved. 'I *knew* there was something. Something big. I couldn't ask because I knew that if you didn't trust me enough to tell me yourself then you didn't feel the same way I did about us.'

'I'll tell you everything,' Adam promised. 'I've got lots of photographs as well.'

They were still holding hands, still engrossed in each other when Miranda's voice interrupted them.

'*Please*, try and keep up. You'll have to stay with the group. I can't leave unauthorised visitors simply wandering around the clinic.'

'Sorry.' Hannah smiled apologetically. She tugged Adam's hand. 'Come on, Adam. This can't take much longer and I did want to see what this place was like.'

They feigned interest in the general labour ward suites and the array of equipment on show. Adam still had hold of one of Hannah's hands as Miranda whisked them quickly past the smaller rooms.

'Costs are considerably down for rooms in this area. A standard birth package will cost no more than a weekend in a good hotel yet the superlative standard of professional care and the same consultants are available should they be required.'

Annie and her husband were still near the back of the group. 'This looks more like us,' he said with satisfaction.

Annie pouted. 'I thought you said we wanted the best.'

'This place is the best. You heard the lady. You get the same consultants and care.'

'I want a spa bath.' Annie's lip trembled. 'And a king-sized bed.'

Miranda was caught in a knot of people who wished to

gain details of prices and booking arrangements. Annie
and her husband were shaping up to have a domestic row
to one side. Somebody else's small child was shrieking
with laughter as he bounced on the single bed in one of
the budget labour rooms. Hannah ignored them all.

'I've been so torn,' she told Adam unhappily, 'between
my love for you and my love for Heidi. I couldn't separate
them but I couldn't bring them together either.'

'I know.' Adam squeezed the hand he was still holding.
'I thought I had it pegged. I thought I could love you and
leave Heidi out of it. Then I got that fright at the playground.'

'What fright?' Hannah asked sharply. 'What happened
at the playground?'

The child bouncing on the bed had been smacked and
was now howling vigorously. Annie was also crying.
Miranda looked as though she would like to cry.

'We'll go out through the solarium,' she announced
wearily. 'You can see the swimming pool and gymnasium
as we go past. The exit to the rose gardens will take you
back to the main entrance and car park. I have brochures
available to everyone who would like more information.'

Hannah and Adam dawdled. The corridor grew quieter
as the group hurried to see the indoor swimming pool.

'What happened at the playground?' Hannah asked
again. She was looking worried.

Adam shook his head. 'It wasn't important.' Then he
smiled wryly. 'Well, it *was* important because it was then
I realised that I loved Heidi as much as I loved you. *I*
couldn't separate things either and I wasn't prepared to
take the risk by admitting it.'

'What risk?'

'The risk of losing you. *And* Heidi. I knew just how
much of a risk I would be taking.'

'You're not going to lose us.' Hannah reached up to touch Adam's cheek. 'That sort of tragedy doesn't happen twice in anyone's lifetime. I know what it's like, too. I lost someone I loved and I'm taking even more of a risk this time.'

'Why?'

'Because my feelings for you are so much stronger than anything I've ever felt before. I didn't even know it was possible to love anyone this much.'

Adam had caught Hannah's hand as it had touched his face. Now he pressed his cheek against it. 'That's exactly how I feel. That's why it made the risk seem even more dangerous.'

'What changed your mind?'

'Something happened today. A case with a baby. I'll tell you all about it later.'

The sound of high heels on the linoleum floor was agitated. Miranda came back into view. '*There* you are. Would you, *please*, come this way? I was about to alert Security.'

'Sorry.' Hannah apologised again. 'We had something important to discuss.'

'We still do.' Adam grinned at Miranda who blinked and then coloured slightly. 'We're having a baby,' he confided.

'Oh! Congratulations.' Miranda almost smiled but then collected herself. 'This way, please.' She glanced back over her shoulder. 'I do hope you'll choose the Cambridge Clinic as your birthing facility.'

'Highly likely.' Adam nodded. 'Don't you think, Hannah?'

'The king-sized bed did look rather inviting,' Hannah murmured. She was holding Adam's hand tightly. He squeezed his agreement. They were passing the swimming pool and gymnasium complex now.

'Are you in the main car park?' Miranda queried briskly.

'Yes,' Hannah said.

'No,' Adam responded simultaneously. Both women glanced at him. 'My transport had to go on another call,' he explained.

'You came here in an ambulance?' Hannah said, amazed. 'Of course—you must have still been on duty. How did you manage that?'

'I made it a priority-one call when your mother told me where you were.'

'What, with lights and sirens?' Hannah was grinning.

'Of course. It was an emergency.'

Hannah laughed. 'I don't think so.'

Miranda was waiting to usher them through the exit. Instead of co-operating, Adam pulled Hannah to a sudden halt and folded his arms around her. 'It was as far as I was concerned,' he said seriously, 'it was a personal emergency.'

Miranda was now listening with open curiosity. 'It appears that you've solved whatever it was that was so urgent.'

'We've made a start,' Adam agreed. He winked at Miranda over Hannah's shoulder. 'We still have a bit of a problem, though.'

'Oh?' Miranda's blush had returned, thanks to the wink. 'What's that?'

'I haven't persuaded Hannah to marry me yet.'

'Oh.' Miranda's smile was making a real effort to break through now. 'Do you think that will take very long? Only I'm supposed to lock up before I go home.'

'That's up to Hannah,' Adam said slowly. 'It's her choice after all.'

Miranda cleared her throat. Now she was grinning broadly. 'What do you say, Hannah?'

Hannah's voice was muffled. Adam couldn't tell whether she was laughing or crying. Her face was still buried against his shoulder. 'No,' she managed, clearly enough. 'I don't think it'll take very long at all.' Hannah lifted her face. 'It's time we went home, Adam. Miranda needs to lock up and we still have a lot to talk about.'

'You haven't said yes yet.' Miranda was now blocking the exit.

'She's right.' Adam gave Hannah an injured glance. 'How could you keep me dangling like this?'

'How can I say yes when you haven't asked me anything?' Hannah pointed out.

'She's right.' Miranda nodded. 'You haven't actually asked the question.'

Adam sighed theatrically. He gave Miranda a conspiratorial look. 'Do I have to go down on my knees?'

'Hmm.' Miranda considered the question. She caught Hannah's glance and grinned again. 'I think we can let you off that bit.'

'Thanks,' Adam muttered. 'Isn't it time you went home, Miranda?'

'I wouldn't this miss this for anything,' Miranda stated. She leaned her back against the exit, keeping it firmly closed. 'Get on with it, Adam.'

Adam put both his hands on Hannah's shoulders, easing her far enough away for him to be able to see her face. His own face stilled as he focused intently, his gaze locked on Hannah's.

'I love you, Hannah. I want to share the rest of my life with you. I want to embrace every moment of joy that being with you will bring. I want to be a father to your daughter and I want to be with you when you bring our child into the world. I want to be with you when our children become parents. And I want to give you as much joy as I know you cannot help but give me.' Adam took a deep, slow breath. 'Will you marry me, Hannah?'

Hannah's grey eyes sparkled with unshed tears. She nodded and sniffed as she spoke. 'Yes, Adam. Of course I will.'

Miranda looked disappointed. 'Is that all you've got to say, Hannah? Adam's speech was beautiful.'

Hannah laughed a little shakily. 'I've got lots of things to say to Adam but we've got plenty of time now.' She glanced up to catch Adam's eye. 'Haven't we?'

He bent and placed a tender kiss on her lips. 'You bet.' Adam smiled broadly enough to create the dimples Hannah loved. 'We've got the rest of our lives,' he told her with enormous satisfaction. 'The emergency is over.'

EPILOGUE

NOTHING had ever felt this good.

The warmth that Hannah Lewis lay basking in had little to do with any sunshine, even though the last rays of a glorious autumn day were still filtering through the windows of her private room in the Cambridge Clinic. The king-sized bed she lay on was neatly made, not having been slept in. The spa pool in the adjoining room hadn't been used either, much to Miranda's obvious disappointment, but Hannah had no intention of sampling any more of the superb birthing and postnatal facilities the Cambridge Clinic had to offer. The attention on her arrival a few hours ago had been more than adequate. While this brief period of rest and solitude was welcome, Hannah was planning to leave any minute now.

Her lips curved slowly into a smile as she opened her eyes. She still couldn't quite believe that she had given birth in the back of an ambulance, with her baby being delivered by his own father! Matt had done his best to get them to the clinic in time, but the background wail of Unit 241's siren had seemed an appropriate way to welcome their son into the world.

Hannah gazed at the tiny face only inches from her own. Edward James Lewis was sound asleep in his Perspex bassinet. Hannah had been left with firm instructions from Miranda to get some sleep herself before Adam returned to take them home, but Hannah was far too happy to sleep. She didn't want to waste a minute of this precious day. There would be plenty of time to rest soon. Her family intended to make sure of that.

Her family. A very contented sigh escaped Hannah's lips. Who would have guessed at how much it would have grown in only the space of a year? Or how close they had all become? Adam's and Hannah's marriage hadn't surprised anyone, but Norma's wedding to Gerry Prescott only weeks later had turned out to be an enormous bonus. Now Heidi and Edward James had a proud grandfather who was as keen as his wife to share in the upbringing of the children. Both Norma and Gerry were encouraging Hannah to return to work just as soon as she wanted to, but Gerry had provided even more than a loving extension to the family.

Formally retiring from general practice to indulge in his long-held passion for wine-making, the older doctor and Norma had moved into a large, well-established vineyard on the outskirts of the city. The generous gift of five acres on the corner of the property bordered by the river had astonished Hannah and Adam and had added a whole new dimension to their future. The whirlwind planning of their dream house had been a joy and the construction was almost complete.

The fabric samples Hannah had been clutching in the shop when her precipitous labour had begun had somehow arrived in Cambridge Clinic with her and now lay abandoned on the end of the bed. The choice had been made for the nursery as soon as Hannah had spotted the rainbow array of teddy bears on the bright yellow background. She had been about to place an order with the shop assistant when her waters had broken and the contractions had started. Hannah had requested an ambulance instead.

The swatch of curtain fabrics fell to the floor seconds

later when an excited small girl clambered onto the bed beside Hannah.

'Mumma!'

'Hello darling,' Hannah gathered Heidi into her arms and smiled over the blonde curls to where Adam was standing. Her own joy was reflected back at her in Adam's expression. Their gazes held and Hannah stretched out one arm to invite Adam closer.

'I came in Daddy's truck,' Heidi announced proudly. 'We've got beds in the back to take you home.'

'You brought the ambulance back?' Hannah's lips curved again even as Adam was kissing her.

'It's got Christmas tree lights.' Heidi bounced out of Hannah's arms and slid backwards off the bed. 'And it makes a *big* noise.'

'Adam—you didn't!'

'Only for a second.' Adam was grinning unrepentantly. 'I figured Heidi deserved to see what her parents did for a living.' His gaze had moved to the bassinet and he reached out to stroke his son's cheek with a gentle touch. 'I guess this wee man's a bit young to appreciate it yet. We'll go home quietly.'

'The siren was the first sound he heard after he was born,' Hannah reminded Adam. She was also grinning. 'We'll probably need one at home to get him off to sleep.'

Heidi had traversed the perimeter of the huge bed and arrived at the side of the bassinet. Her eye level was directly in line with the baby's face and her breath clouded the Perspex as her blue eyes examined her brother carefully. Finally she reached over the side and touched Edward's thatch of soft, dark hair. Heidi's brow furrowed as she transferred her gaze to Adam.

'He's got Daddy's hair,' she exclaimed indignantly. 'Why haven't I?'

'You've got Mummy's hair.' Adam smiled. 'And that's the way it should be.'

'Why?' Heidi was still staring at Adam. 'Is it 'cos I'm a girl?'

'No.' Adam's tone was loving. 'It's because you're Heidi and you're perfect just the way you are,'

Hannah wasn't surprised at the prickle of tears forming in her eyes. She had often been caught by the depth of the bond between her daughter and her husband in the last few months. Hannah nestled into Adam's arms and blinked the tears away as she, too, gazed at the baby who represented a new bond that could only link their family even more closely.

'His name is Edward,' Hannah told Heidi, 'Because that's Daddy's middle name and it was his father's name, too.'

'Ed... Ed...' Heidi found the name difficult despite the recent improvement in her speech. 'Eddie.' Her face crinkled thoughtfully and then lit up with a grin. 'Teddy!' she said triumphantly.

Adam laughed. 'Some people do call Edwards Teddy,' he agreed.

Heidi's grin widened. 'Does he queek?'

'Not yet,' Hannah said hurriedly.

'When he's bigger,' Adam added firmly, 'I'm sure he'll squeak just like you.'

'And teddy.' Heidi's interest in the baby had clearly faded for the moment. 'Daddy?'

'What's up, button?'

'I want to go home now.'

Adam's arm tightened around Hannah. His gaze took on the thoughtful intensity that Hannah loved. Her answer to whatever question was coming would be of the utmost importance to him.

'Are you ready? Adam asked with concern. 'Do you feel well enough to come home with us now?'

'And Teddy.' Heidi sounded worried. 'We've got to take him home, too?'

'Of course we do. And I've never felt better,' Hannah said with assurance. Her smile at Adam wobbled just a little as fresh tears of joy threatened briefly. 'Let's *all* go home.'

MILLS & BOON®

Makes any time special™

Mills & Boon publish 29 new titles
every month. Select from...

Modern Romance™   Tender Romance™

Sensual Romance™

Medical Romance™ Historical Romance™

MAT2

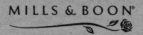

Medical Romance™

ACCIDENTAL RENDEZVOUS *by Caroline Anderson*

Audley Memorial Series

Audley A&E is an emotional place, but Sally is not prepared for the emotions Nick Baker stirs when he comes back into her life. He's been searching for her for seven years, and for all that time Nick's unknowingly been a father…

ADAM'S DAUGHTER *by Jennifer Taylor*

Part 1 of A Cheshire Practice

Nurse Elizabeth Campbell *had* to tell Dr Adam Knight that he was the father of her sister's child. He was furious that no one told him he had a daughter and was determined to be in her life — only that meant he was in Beth's life too. This fuelled their attraction, but were his feelings really for her, or for her sister?

THE DOCTOR'S ENGAGEMENT *by Sarah Morgan*

Holly Foster has been best friends with GP Mark Logan since childhood, so when he asked her to pretend to be his fiancée, how could she refuse? One searing kiss was all it took to make Holly realise that being Mark's fiancée was very different to being his friend!

On sale 7th September 2001

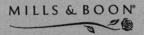

MILLS & BOON®

Medical Romance™

A NURSE TO TRUST by Margaret O'Neill

With a painful relationship behind him, Dr Dan Davis
doesn't want to place his emotions in the hands of
Clare Summers, his new practice nurse at the mobile
surgery. He has learnt to trust her nursing skills; will
he ever be able to trust her with his heart?

THE DEVOTED FATHER by Jean Evans

Kate Jameson is beginning to make GP Nick Forrester
wonder if he has made a mistake by not allowing
himself to love again since his little daughter's mother
left. Maybe Kate's love is something they both need, if
only he can find the courage to make them a family.

A SPANISH PRACTICE by Anne Herries

The warmth of the Mediterranean sun was causing Dr
Jenny Talforth to blossom in front of Miguel's eyes,
and he was finding it harder to resist his attraction to
her. But resist he must, because he had commitments
– and she was clearly escaping from something—or
someone…

On sale 7th September 2001

*Available at most branches of WH Smith, Tesco,
Martins, Borders, Easons, Sainsbury, Woolworth
and most good paperback bookshops* 0801/03b

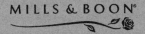

ARE YOU A FAN
OF MILLS & BOON®
MEDICAL ROMANCES™?

If YOU are a regular United Kingdom buyer of
Mills & Boon Medical Romances we would welcome
your opinion on the books we publish.

Harlequin Mills & Boon have a Reader Panel for
Medical Romances. Each person on the panel
receives a questionnaire every third month asking for
their opinion of the books they have read in the past
three months. Everyone who sends in their replies
will have a chance of winning ONE YEAR'S FREE
Medicals, sent by post—48 books in all.

If you would like to be considered for inclusion on
the Panel please give us details about yourself below.
All postage will be free. Younger readers are
particularly welcome.

Year of birth.............................Month..........................

Age at completion of full-time education.....................

Single ❑   Married ❑   Widowed ❑   Divorced ❑

Your name (print please)..

Address..

....Postcode ....

Thank you! Please put in envelope and post to:
HARLEQUIN MILLS & BOON READER PANEL,
FREEPOST SF195, PO BOX 152, SHEFFIELD S11 8TE